STRIKE

THE NEW PROTECTORATE STORIES: VOLUME THREE

ABIGAIL KELLY

Author's Note

Strike is a standalone novella within the wider *New Protectorate Series* and can be read as such. However, it does contain some spoilers for other books in the series. A full reading list and character directory can be found at abigailkkelly.com. Content warnings can also be found there, as well as in backmatter of this book, alongside a glossary.

~Abigail

For those who love to wander
within and without,
go far.

CHAPTER ONE

DECEMBER 2044 - THE ELVISH PROTECTORATE

SHE WAS ONCE BOUNDLESS.

It was the only way she could describe her life before the storm, and the dragon, and *newness.*

She was immeasurable, her consciousness a gossamer veil between the horizon and the dome of stars; formless, with neither body nor true mind, but *presence,* personhood all the same.

Consciousness did not come all at once. It grew over eons, in starts and stops, and not always in isolation. In quiet moments, she thought she could reach deep into her memory, to that wild primordial time, and touch other beginnings, other beings, who joined to become *her.*

Her first clear thought came as a surprise. She had no eyes, no ears, no body at all, and yet she sensed the world below her and felt the thought in every part of her being. It was fully-formed, a strike of electricity through a haze of dull awareness: *What is that?*

More thoughts came, each one quicker, more focused than the last. Existing as magic and thought, she could do little more than watch the world below her and *hunger.* For what, she didn't know — at least, not for many, many years. How could she, when she did not have words for the concept of curiosity? For loneliness? Despair?

And yet she felt, and wondered, and decided that if ever there was a chance to be reborn into something else, she would trade her vastness for even a moment of *life*. Drifting over the world, she watched those below and felt envy. It took many thousands of years for her to recognize that they, too, were beings with thoughts. Watching them closely revealed previously unimaginable differences between them.

Sound. Movement. Community. *Change.*

They did not make sense to her, but one day she began to wish she could know what it was like to be small and strange and together with others. There was no one to hear her silent pleas, but she wished anyway.

It came as something of a shock, however, when that wish came true.

After eons as an entity of pure power, limitless and yet never free, she did not expect to feel herself... compressed. *Squeezed.* Like the claps of thunder she knew so well, the feeling rocked her. Once, twice, a third time. Again and again, faster, harder, until she was utterly insensible with confusion and fear and a brutal sort of pain that she had no name for.

Pain was the first thing her body felt, quickly followed by the foreign bite of cold, and finally a curious sensation like a string was attached to her belly and pulling tighter every second.

Her body, so strange and new, ripped apart in a flash before it came back together again. Weightless and then weighted. Bursting and then resewn. Made and unmade.

The fact that she had a body at all was impossible to comprehend. The knowledge was there, as real and solid as her flesh, but she could not process it at once — or at all as her form compressed and then shredded itself again in a blaze of white hot agony. Muscle roped new bone, sinew stretched, and then they were unraveled, the bone crushed to pulp, the muscle stripped strand by strand, her sinews pulled taut until they, too, snapped.

The agony was unimaginable. She had never felt pain, nor comfort. She did not know what it was to be battered and healed again. Was this life? Was this what she had hoped for?

It can't just be this! It can't be this!

The world spun. Then *sound*.

Oh, sound! It rose in volume as she tumbled through the cold, hair whipping, a silent scream torn from lips which had never spoken a word.

Terror. That was what she felt as she fell from the sky. Lightning cut jagged streaks around her, flashing through the thin skin of her eyelids. It kissed her flesh even as she plunged to the world she had longed to be part of for so long.

Impact. A powerful force rattled her frame. Teeth clacked together and spots floated in front of her eyes as she tumbled faster, this time with more weight, until shadows stretched out around her with a *snap!*

She slowed. The world stopped spinning. The awful, taut feeling in her middle began to dissipate. Gradually, she became aware of new sensations: something rough against her skin, warmth, and a rich, spicy scent.

Before she could silently ask all her usual *hows* and *whys*, there was another jarring *thump,* and then stillness.

Her ears rang. Distantly, she heard sounds and felt the lack of icy wind, but her mind was muddled, her usual curiosity muffled by discomfort and that terrible fear. She squeezed her eyes shut and curled closer to the warmth — her own personal sun, who banished the wind and the fear with ease.

Lightning flashed, but then she perceived a deeper darkness all around her. Even the sounds were muffled. Only the rasp of her own strange breathing and someone else's filled the small, warm space.

Something curled around the delicate bones of her ankle, and though her head swam, she *had* to see. To know she had an ankle at all was so baffling that it could not be overlooked. Her eyes popped open to peer down, but her vision was immediately filled with something else entirely.

A face stared down at her in the soft darkness. Four horns were a proud crown. A wide nose tapered into high cheekbones and an angular chin. A soft mouth was ever-so-slightly parted, revealing white teeth and fangs. But the eyes—

Half-lidded eyes of shadowed green stared down at her with a look she couldn't hope to decipher. They were lined with long, spiky lashes, and when they roved over her face, she felt... *she felt.*

All was still again, but this time it was *inside.* For just a moment, she was no longer spinning, falling, crashing together and pulling apart. She was simply *held.*

A rumble startled her. Lightning flashed again — from her this time. It burst from her skin in a series of bright, colorful flashes. Magenta. Apple green. Sunny yellow. A blue so bright, it was practically white.

She stared down at her body with a numb sort of surprise. Its pearlescent skin and flesh, glowing faintly even when the sparks died down, seemed unaccountably strange to her. She had seen so many bodies over the eons and she had dreamed of a miracle, where she might have one of her own, but now that it was a reality, she wasn't entirely sold on it.

The being who stared at her made a chuffing sound before he showed her all of his teeth. He rumbled again, but this time it was quieter, and it did not startle her as much because she realized it was coming from the warmth she was pressed against. *Him.*

I don't understand you, she thought, suddenly wild and afraid again. *Oh, I want to understand you!*

If she could not communicate, what was the point of being bound in flesh? If her muscles burned and her skin crawled, each nerve raw with its newness, why should she want a body?

Her fingers spasmed against the hard plating of her rescuer's chest. *Am I defective?*

She made another high noise. Pain prickled every nerve and

crushing disappointment made it hard to breathe the air she had never needed before.

Pressure surrounded her as he dropped his head down, close enough for her to feel warm breath on her cheeks. That coil around her ankle — she had an *ankle!* — tightened, too.

He rumbled again. His lips moved slowly, but still she could not understand him. Why not? Was she broken?

She opened her mouth, desperate for *something* to happen, but could only make a high noise of distress.

His expression darkened. Heavy brows snapped together as his rumbling ceased. Gently, he put pressure on her head until her nose pressed against the hot skin of his throat. When she was there, he spoke again, soft and slow, until she began to calm.

Again and again, she heard the same words, though it would take her a year to understand what they meant.

You're safe, he said. *I have you now, my fallen star.*

CHAPTER TWO

THEY NAMED HER HELE.

Heh-lay. It was the first word she learned how to pronounce, and it meant *light.* Her second word was *why.*

Constantin and Valerie, the recent empty-nesters who had taken on responsibility for her care, liked to joke that with her ravenous curiosity and habit of getting into trouble, she should have been born a cat shifter. Her hunger for knowledge was endless, and her rapidfire questions often surprised the dragons she met.

As curious as a cat, they lovingly teased. *And as temperamental, too.*

Hele didn't quite get the joke, but that didn't bother her. Her relief at simply being able to *understand* them outweighed any slight she might have felt.

She remembered those first few days after her fall, when her Isand and the dragons claimed her as their own. The trip to the Draakonriik, what she came to learn was the dragon's territory in the wider United Territories and Allies, was a blur of raw nerves and panic. They tried to communicate with her, but she could not understand or reciprocate. The more she tried, the more distressed she became, until Vael, the dragon who caught her, barked something in his low voice and hid her in his wings again.

She only felt peace in the shelter he provided.

He held her in his lap, strong arms banded around her trembling, unstable frame, the entire trip. When they eventually made it to the Roost, he still did not leave her side. Vael was the one who first discovered she did not need to eat more than once every few weeks. It was Vael who wrapped her in blankets and sat with her in a dark room until she settled. It was Vael who helped the Isand find a home for her — Taevas's own uncle, Constantin and his Chosen, Valerie.

At first, she did not know what to make of him. Or any of the dragons, really.

Who were these strange beings? She thought she knew, once. Hele knew the shape of a dragon's wings in the sky. She knew their roar and their blue flame. Over eons, she had seen them take their first flights and plunge to their deaths.

So she knew what they *were*, but when she was her other self, they had seemed so small. Now they were mostly much bigger than she was. They were mind bogglingly complex. Their language was both beautiful and contradictory, their habits strange, their culture grown over countless generations she had watched come and go.

If she thought that she would be able to understand them simply because she had a body, Hele was sorely mistaken. Often she did not understand *anything* they did.

Just about the only thing that came naturally to her was flying, or *wandering*, as she called it. When she escaped into her other form, she and the dragons were in perfect sync. Her family marveled at her as she dashed across the sky — little more than a splash of color and light. They crowed with laughter when she accidentally triggered a rainshower, and they told anyone who would listen about how fast she could zip from one end of the lake to the other.

In flight, Hele was a natural. In the rest... she was less so.

Life, she quickly understood, was stranger than she could have imagined. It involved a thousand tiny decisions made in a second, context gleaned from a lifetime of conditioning, and the ability to read the people who existed around her.

She had no skill with any of it. Sometimes, in those early days, when she could not speak fluently, couldn't understand what was happening around her, and struggled to withstand the bombardment of sensation that was life on the ground, Hele despaired.

Had she been created broken? Was that why she could not read an expression, articulate a thought, easily traverse the culture she found herself in?

Some days, she hid in the room her family had given her, her eyes squeezed shut as she tried to will herself into a different shape — something *better*. Other days, she dematerialized and was a streak of light, free of structure for a moment before the loneliness came back with force.

Because, for all that she was often overwrought and confused, Hele *liked* her dragons.

She did not have a concept of kindness until they treated her with it. She did not know love until they welcomed her into the clan with open wings. She did not know acceptance until her adopted mother sat with her on the edge of the perch attached to their roost and drew her strange new daughter into her arms as if she had always held claim to that sacred space.

She did not know longing, *true* longing, until she met Vael. And she would not trade any of that for a return to the infinite.

So she adapted.

Despair would not defeat her. Hele would not allow herself to squander the opportunity she had been given. If she wanted to speak to the people around her, to know her new world, then she had to find a way to do it.

Her family quickly organized a tutor to teach her their language — an eclectic mix of English, Estonian, and an ancient dragonish tongue that, though long dead, still shadowed much of their formal dealings. The formal teaching was only a supplement to her constant observation of those around her, however. She listened to everything, she mouthed the words until they made sense, and she found a way to get her answers when those new syllables failed her. She *learned.*

It was a huge relief to discover that she could, in fact, pick up the words easily. There was nothing *wrong* with her other than ignorance borne of newness. Though the dragons were shocked by the speed at which she learned, Hele felt herself moving at a glacial pace.

How can I live if I cannot ask questions? If I cannot know these people?

The process was often frustrating, embarrassing, and seemed to stall more than accelerate, but she forced herself through every barrier that presented itself with pure, electrified will.

It took six months for her to gain fluency, and then another six to adequately master reading and writing. Every spare moment was spent bent over a tablet, studying until her eyes blurred, and since she did not sleep, spare moments were plentiful.

It helped that her family treated her no differently than anyone else. They talked to her constantly, made space for her in their lives automatically, and pushed her to try new things.

They accepted her, and guided her, and when the time was right, they formally made her a member of Clan Aždaja.

She only had a few broken sentences at her disposal when her Isand, the formidable Taevas, threw a small party in the garden below his massive spire in her honor. She had been with them three months.

She had been nervous around so many unknown faces — dragons of the Clan, their mates, children, guards, *Vael* — but her family had been there, and her pride was a living thing, and she would not shame herself by shrinking before the crowd.

So she walked naked to meet her Isand on his polished wood throne, a relic from the Old Country, and she met his gaze steadily when he raised her chin with a single claw. A smile kicked up one corner of his mouth, deepening the laugh line there, when her nervousness transmuted into sparks that danced between them.

"You are strong and unique," he told her, eyes dancing in the light of the blue dragonfire that wreathed his throne. "You are not a dragon, but you have a dragon's pride, a dragon's strength." His violet eyes slid over her shoulder for an instant before they came back to her, sly. "You have a dragon's heart. You are a *flawless* addition to this clan."

Though she only understood every third or fourth word, Hele felt a great, throbbing tenderness for her Isand. She knew what he meant. *I am accepted.*

She could feel all the eyes of the clan on her naked back when he announced, "I, Taevas Aždaja, Isand of the Draakonriik and leader of the Aždaja clan, welcome you, our beautiful Hele, to our family. May you bring honor to our name and burn bright enough for all to see."

Her eyes fluttered shut as he leaned forward, close enough to kiss, and breathed out a puff of ice cold, blue flame. It danced along her lips, her cheeks, her nose, the paper-thin skin of her eyelids, before it vanished, leaving only a prickling sort of cold in its wake.

Taevas pressed the lightest, skimming kiss to her lips before he straightened once more. He looked proud and terrifying in the blue light. Broad-shouldered, dressed in richly embroidered silk and velvet, his horns a menacing arch over a head of long, black hair, he was the most magnificent dragon she had ever seen.

But he did not make her heart race, or her mind quiet, or the world stop spinning. Only *one* dragon did that.

When he grasped her shoulders and spun her around to face the crowd, he boomed, "Welcome our newest clanmate: *Hele Varvaara Aždaja!*"

And then her dragons threw back their heads and roared with welcome. Fire danced, alcohol flowed, well-wishers pressed kisses to her cheeks and babies flew clumsily into her lap for attention.

Her clan rejoiced. Some dark ache she had carried for eons began to ease.

All the while, her dark-eyed dragon stood on the fringe of the merriment, his wings back and his gaze, proud and full of warmth, locked on her. He was not Clan Aždaja, but the fluttering in her stomach told her he belonged to her anyway.

~

Days passed. Months. Then a year. Every moment she lived, her time as something *more* got dimmer, the eons of memory sifting away like ash on the wind. She settled, and grew, and she began to yearn again.

With the clan's influence, she often felt far more *dragon* than elemental. Mostly that was a good thing, but sometimes she chafed under the rules and social structure that felt foreign to her very core.

Her need for independence increased every day. She lacked the same instincts as the dragons and often did not understand why they did certain things like staying in one place all their lives, or rigorously following a clan hierarchy. Occasionally her family looked at her like they were as baffled by her as she was by them, but it was not often enough to make her feel like an outsider.

She was a member of Clan Aždaja. She was dragonkin, accepted by the Isand himself, and she loved the baffling culture she had been adopted into.

Though she didn't see him as often as she would like, Hele was delighted to receive regular gifts from Vael. He sent books he thought she would enjoy to her tablet. He had pale blue blankets — fire retardant, of course — delivered to her after her first flight with Taevas. For her birthday, he escorted her to the Roost's library and watched her read, a lopsided smile on his deep green face. He didn't speak much, but that didn't bother her. She spoke enough for the both of them. Besides, his quiet was relaxing — an extension of that stillness she craved.

He was a perfect complement to her riotous thoughts and impulses; a strong hand that held her tethered, lest she shoot off into the lonely expanse once more.

It took her a year and six months to understand that the warmth she felt for her personal sun was not the same as what she felt for her family. It was... different.

Brighter. Hotter.

She wanted to see him more, but he was busy working as one of Taevas's bodyguards, so their paths rarely crossed. When she did manage to catch a glimpse of him, she felt a curious weightlessness, like the moment before she let go of her physical form, except not. It was a new feeling. She *liked* it.

One year, eight months, and two weeks from her fall, Hele stood in the doorway of the family dwelling and watched as Constantin swept his Chosen into his wings and kissed her. She watched, and she blinked, and she thought, *I want Vael to do that.*

And then everything began to spin again.

CHAPTER THREE

MAY 2047 - DRUMMOND ISLAND, THE
DRAAKONRIIK

"I WANT MY OWN ROOST."

Constantin, a huge royal purple dragon with laugh lines and
an abundance of salt and pepper curls, looked up from his tablet
to meet her gaze. Valerie sat beside him on the low sofa that
spanned most of the sunken living space, sipping a cup of tea and
looking utterly unsurprised.

Constantin lowered his tablet to rest on his knee. "Pardon?"

Hopping deftly over the back of the couch, Hele landed in the
center of the seating area, her feet bare and her expression determined. "I want my own roost. Like Alex. I want to be like her."

Valerie, a deep, deep red to complement her Chosen's purple,
set her mug down on the coffee table before she held out a clawed
hand. Out of habit, Hele grasped it and let her mother reel her in.
Sparks jumped from Hele to Valerie, but her tough dragon skin
had no trouble handling the tiny bites of electricity — unlike
some electronics, and a number of ill-fated dresses she made the
mistake of purchasing from non-dragon owned businesses.

"*Minu tütar,*" her mother crooned, "where is this coming from? Your *isa* and I have only had you in the nest for two years. I knew this would come, but I thought we had more time."

"Alexandra is much older than you, sweet," her father chimed in, brow furrowed and lips tight. "You cannot expect to be like her so soon. She is sixty years old."

Hele jutted her chin out. "I am *thousands.*"

Valerie squeezed her hand. "Yes, this is true, but there is still so much you don't know about the world. What if you don't like living on your own? I worry about you being lonely, *tütar.*"

She had learned so much in the two years since her fall, but had yet to master patience. Hele felt her hair spark and sizzle, the ends of the long, shifting strands dissolving into electricity as her temper began to fray.

Don't lose your head, she heard Alex, their other daughter, say. *If you want something, you have to keep your cool. Exploding into sparks will just make it easier to not take you seriously.*

Alex always had good advice, so Hele did her best to listen to her. She was confident and, at least to her untrained eye, worldly. It was Alex who took her shopping. It was Alex who showed her all the best sunning spots around the lake. It was Alex who taught her how to use her tablet, and introduced her to fun books about love and sex and tragedy.

Hele looked at Alex and didn't just admire her for her swagger, but for her *life.* Alex lived life how it pleased her. She had her own roost. She took home lovers and flew high without supervision. She did not need things explained, nor to be coddled.

While Hele knew her situation was based entirely on her needs — she *did* need questions answered, to be coddled, to have a family — she was ready to take her next steps into the life she had only dreamed of.

Independence. Fun. Responsibility. Duty to the clan. Love.

Vael.

"I will not be lonely," Hele assured them. "I will still see you, yes? If I have a roost, I can come back like Alex and Artem do."

Though she felt fairly sure, there was a wavering note of uncertainty in her voice. It happened that sometimes she made assumptions. Had she made another assumption that when she left the nest she would still be their *tütar,* one of their offspring like her brother and sister? They often left for long stretches of time. Alex lived with the other single dragons on the mainland, and Artem had a Chosen and his own mountain in the Elvish Protectorate. They both came back to their family nest often. Would it be different for her?

Constantin set his tablet aside and reached out to grasp her free hand. His fingers were large and wickedly clawed. She always felt small compared to her family, though she knew that she towered over many other people in the world. "Sweet, of course you will always have a place in the nest. You belong to us. You know this."

A tight ball of anxiety began to unwind in her chest. The dragons had accepted her as one of their own without question, but still, she wondered about her place. "All right, *Isa.* "

"We don't want to cage you," Valerie chimed in. "You are independent and your own person. You should live how you want to. We just worry that such an upheaval so soon might not be good for you."

Hele had a peculiar realization then: it was entirely possible to love her adopted family more than she ever had, and yet still want to leave them. The feelings, which had previously seemed mutually exclusive, were perfectly in sync. She loved them so much that her throat tightened with the force of it, but she also knew that she was right. It was time to spread her wings.

"I need to do this. It's important to me." Her words were soft, her cadence still slightly unnatural, but the feeling was strong.

Her parents, who had taken her into their nest and treated her like a daughter without hesitation, shared a meaningful look. "All right," Constantin answered, his expression bittersweet. "We'll help you find a roost, but I want to see you in the nest every week, so I know you're well."

Hele's heart raced. A smile curved her mouth. "Of course, *Isa*. I will still need company when I do the crossword."

He'd been in a piss-poor mood for five days. It just so happened that it had also been five days since he last saw his star.

A year ago, the other dragons in the Wing might have given him shit for his bad attitude, knowing that it stemmed from his entirely obvious obsession with a certain elemental, but they had long since exchanged jokes for pitying glances.

Two years. Two years had crawled by since he caught his falling star, his curious, delightfully strange Hele, and that deeply *dragon* part of his brain simply... *clicked.*

This one is mine, he'd thought, perfectly calm even as they plunged through the air. *This is who I Choose.*

Gods, he'd been so excited to hold her in his arms, to stare down at her shining face in the shade of his wings. His heart soared when she blinked up at him with wonder. *"I've always thought lightning was pretty,"* he remembered saying. *"And now I get to hold it in my arms."*

But she hadn't understood him. She couldn't speak. She could only panic, and his heart had sunk.

He'd Chosen her, but he could not claim her — not until she was ready.

It wasn't such a hardship at first. Getting her settled and cared for was the first step. Watching her grow, and learn, and blow everyone away with her intelligence was a privilege he wouldn't have given up for anything.

He Chose her when she fell into his arms. He *loved* her when she flourished.

So he was in the running for the longest a dragon in the Wing had waited to claim his Chosen. Vael was just behind Pasha, who had spent the better part of five years hunting for a nameless elvish woman, and poor, mad Radek, who refused to believe the mate he'd lost in the final days of the war was truly dead. He'd gone damn near feral in the one hundred and thirty years since.

A glimpse of my future.

A dragon did not wait. It went against every instinct they possessed. Waiting meant that their Chosen might be unprotected, left alone in the cold without a roost or the shelter of their mate's wings, or *worse* — they could be claimed by another.

Impossible.

His entire being balked at the thought. Instinct was a roaring pressure on taut nerves. The longer he waited, the worse it got. The temptation to clutch Hele in his claws and take her away grew every day. Always a quiet man, Vael became downright *surly* as the months passed. His mood only darkened when his comrades began to worry about him.

"Just claim her," Radek had bluntly advised him. *"Don't wait and watch her slip from your claws. You'll regret it, boy."*

But she wasn't ready.

The only impulse that could outpace possessiveness in a dragon was the absolutely immutable urge to *protect*. Hele's health and happiness were above all things in his priorities. In a normal mating, the desire to claim would go hand in hand with the need to protect, but for them...

Hele was so young. Though she looked like a grown woman and he knew intellectually that she was ancient, he could not forget the heartrending vulnerability and fear of her first few days earthside. He thought of how she'd clutched at him in the dark, her body shaking, and the confidence he had watched bloom like a flower in the sun. *Soon,* he tried to reassure himself. *Soon she'll be ready.*

But soon wasn't soon enough, and every day he felt like he was a step closer to snapping.

Add onto that constant tension the fact that he hadn't seen her or heard from her in five days? Vael was a bomb about to detonate.

"Go home." Taevas, the man who had saved his life so many

years ago and the Isand he would follow into the Underworld if necessary, wiggled his claws in the direction of the Roost. They were standing on the tarmac of his personal landing strip. A sleek black m-jet loomed over their shoulders, recently emptied of the Isand and his Wing.

Though they all could have flown to the New Zone — where they suffered through a week of United Congress meetings — without the help of technology, Taevas liked to be able to work while traveling. That meant his m-jet was more of a luxe floating office than a plane.

Officially, it was every member of the Wing's job to guard the Isand every moment he was not in his roost. There were four dragons in the Wing. Two were charged with keeping their eyes on the Isand at all times while the other two scouted ahead and behind.

A man whose duty meant everything to him, Vael immediately answered his Isand with a flat negative. "I'll see you back to the Roost."

The sun was setting over their heads, though it was tucked behind a thick layer of clouds. The light brushed Taevas's deep purple skin with soft yellows and pinks when he glibly replied, "I'm your fucking Isand. If I tell you to go home, you *go home.*"

Vael glared. "I'm *fine.*"

"You're not. You've been practically coming out of your skin since we left." Taevas strode over to the narrow escalator that wound around one of the towers built solely for a perch. The rest of his Wing followed suit, their eyes carefully averted from Vael.

He gritted his teeth.

Pulling his phone out of his pocket, Taevas casually checked his notifications as they climbed up and up, toward the perch. He looked at it for a second, smirked, then quickly typed out a message. That done, he cast a look over his shoulder and said, "I'm giving you a week off, Vael. Starting immediately. Go. *Home.*"

He knew that tone. Taevas was serious, and that meant there was absolutely no arguing with him. Vael could only nod, his pride and his duty and his relentless urgency all tangled up into a knot in his throat.

Go home.

They both knew he didn't mean the roost he'd purchased on a small spit of land just a short flight away from Drummond Island last year.

Go home to Hele.

But he couldn't. She still lived in the family nest, where she was safe and cared for but inaccessible to him. He could not fly home because his home, the person instinct recognized as *true north*, did not yet know how much he needed her.

Vael felt a deep, painful exhaustion settle into his bones as he watched his Isand and comrades throw themselves off of the perch one by one. Their wings extended with a snap as they caught an air current and arrowed back toward Drummond Island.

Gods, what he wouldn't do to simply *hold* her. He was so goddamn touch hungry, he felt like there were ants under his skin. He hadn't slept properly in two years for the lack of her in his arms. Food tasted like ash unless she was with him, wrinkling her nose with playful disgust from across the table.

He missed her in a way that felt deeper than simple separation. He missed the things they had yet to have, and that was almost worse.

Short, spiky hair moving in the brisk wind, Vael stepped up to the edge of the perch and stared into the blush colored horizon. He was embarrassed that he'd been dismissed — and forced on *vacation*, of all things — but he knew that his Isand was right. He needed a break.

I need *to see her.*

If he couldn't touch her, tuck her into the shelter of his wings, fucking kiss her until he couldn't breathe, then at least he might be able to sit with her for a while and listen to her talk about everything he'd missed while he was gone. It wasn't the same, but it was enough.

Vael leapt off of the perch. *It has to be enough.*

Chapter Four

Her nest was more of a studio apartment in the great, arch-shaped honeycomb that was the roost in De Tour Village, but it was *hers*.

Hele relished the thought as she walked to the sliding glass door that opened up onto her perch. Like the Dragon Roost on Drummond Island, home to the Isand and center of the 'Riik's government, it was designed to accommodate those who traveled primarily by wing. The building was an open arch, with a flourishing garden, business center, and m-lev hub in its center. The apartments within the arch faced one another, allowing for socialization as neighbors hopped from perch to perch. The perches — balconies that could withstand the weight of a full grown dragon — lacked railings, the nests were large, and the ceilings tall. What it lacked in square footage, it made up for in comfort.

Hele *loved* it. The apartment itself was not particularly noteworthy, and truthfully she felt more *at home* outside and out of her skin than inside, but she was delighted by what the new development represented: control over her own life.

Though the first few days were disorienting without the noise and motion of her family, she felt a heady sense of relief in having her own space, her independence. It had begun to pain her that she did not know any other elementals, but from what she had read, Hele came to the conclusion that her kind were not keen on living by other people's rules or routines. The word she came by most often was *mercurial.*

This impression came mostly from her single most read book: the newly released *The Shrouded City* by Elise Sasini. Part memoir, part love story, part biography, it was a sensational new release that exposed the hitherto unconfirmed guardian of San Francisco, *Calamity,* a fog elemental. Hele was obsessed with his story and horrified by it in equal measure.

He did not know what a home was, she thought, skimming her hand over the plain wall beside the door. *He did not know love, or family, or comfort. He was born in violence and pain. I was saved from that. I am loved.*

So why did she feel such a nagging *lack?*

Suddenly restless, Hele waved her hand over the small sensor by the door. The glass panel slid away from the octagonal doorway. Her apartment was not on the interior of the building, so she didn't stare out across the arch and into another person's dwelling. Instead, she was positioned on the outside of the arch, which gave her a marvelous view of the stretch of frothy water between De Tour and the Dragon Roost.

The sun was setting. The sky was overcast, but the light that filtered through the clouds was blush colored and streaked with burnt orange. The air whipping off the water was cold and faintly wet. She felt it bite into the bare skin of her feet and gust up under her long, gauzy skirt.

Shapes criss-crossed the horizon, and calls echoed — whistles, mostly, but also the occasional bone-rattling dragon roar.

Her eyes, black like spilled oil, scanned the horizon. She held her breath.

Was he there? Was he one of those massive shadows against the clouds? She knew the shape of his wings, the very particular way he twitched his tail. Hele could spot Vael from miles away. She *had.* Many of her days had been spent with her legs over the edge of the perch, watching, waiting, for a glimpse of an emerald-hued dragon.

That is what's missing, she thought, angular brows drawing together. Her hair, snowy white with an undertone of lavender and long enough to brush the backs of her calves, swayed in the wind. *This dwelling is empty without my Chosen.*

That's what Valerie used to say when Constantin would leave for a day or two, fulfilling his role as a member of Taveas's council. When Hele was still new, her English rudimentary and her knowledge of relationships even worse, she asked what it was that Valerie and Constantin were, what a *Chosen* was.

"A Chosen is a dragon's mate," her mother explained, raking her claws through Hele's fall of hair in soothing strokes. *"A mate is someone you love differently than a friend, or a clanmate. They are both of those things, but also more. For a dragon, a Chosen is someone you wish to be with above all others, for the rest of your lives. You only Choose once, and when you do, that person becomes the center of your world."*

She'd gone on to explain nesting, offspring, sex, and other intimacies that Hele struggled to wrap her head around. Still, Vael's face lingered in her mind during the entire conversation. She remembered him staring down at her in the dark. His proud horns. His sharp teeth. The spicy scent of him and the soft rumble of his voice.

Hele thought of the days when he held her *constantly.* He had not done so since she joined her family. He hadn't so much as grazed her with a claw, or curled his tail around her ankle. He *certainly* hadn't enclosed her in his wings again, which she now understood to be a startlingly intimate thing to do. Only mates and offspring were trusted with a dragon's embrace.

He must want me as a mate, she told herself as she slipped the straps of her dress off of her narrow shoulders. *He embraced me. I want him to do it again.*

Now that she had her own nest, her own dwelling, she would Choose him. It was time to *live,* and the part of life she desperately wanted to experience was romantic love. She wanted that intimacy. She wanted that feeling of safety and stillness she so briefly experienced. She was ravenously curious about sex, and she wanted to explore the subject with only one dragon.

Her dress slid down her body to pool around her feet. As usual, she wore nothing underneath. Hele loved the billowy feeling of a long dress, but her skin crawled when she attempted to wear anything tighter.

Kicking the loose fabric back into the apartment, she took a moment to simply stand there on her perch, her skin bare and her lungs full of cold, wet air.

The only way this would be better was if Vael were here.

Shaking off the thought, she padded her way over to the edge of the perch. Her apartment was on the fiftieth floor. Staring down at the grounds made her stomach drop, but in the delicious, exhilarating way that all beings who soared the sky not only loved, but chased.

A thought, a burst of magic as easy and natural as an exhale, and she was released from her physical form.

Hele streaked across the sky. She bounced between the low-slung clouds, darkening them even as electricity snapped in her wake. It was not quite the same as the vastness of before, but it was close.

She tended to lose track of time when she wandered, so it did not surprise her that when she spotted the flash of a familiar wing, darkened with the dragonish nocturnal pigment shift that disguised them against the night sky, the warm colors of sunset had long faded.

Her heart did not race at the sight of Vael's massive form cutting through the clouds because she did not have one. Instead, her exhilaration came through as a flurry of lightning strikes all around him. They grazed his powerful body like illuminated fingertips.

A powerful, arrow-shaped head lifted, peering up into the

clouds. His wings extended and pushed forward, briefly halting his momentum just long enough to look around.

Overjoyed at the sight of her mate, Hele dove around him, her body just a smear of light against the roiling clouds.

A familiar, rumbling chuff was her greeting. It was perhaps slightly rougher than normal, but she didn't think anything of it. When he lifted a foreclaw to indicate she should follow him down to the craggy shore, she didn't hesitate.

He landed before she did. Weighing several tons, Vael's shifted- form hit the rocky shore with a tree-rattling *thwump!*

Hele touched the ground much more gently. With a thought, she arrowed down and, a second before she reached the rocks, her form coalesced into flesh once more. Her skin glowed in the dark like the lingering flash of a lightning bolt. It didn't bother her that she was bare before him. Dragons often wore nothing at all, since most people didn't go through the hassle and expense of having their clothing woven with sigils, allowing them to disappear and reappear with a shift.

When her magnificent dragon changed his form, she was a little disappointed to see that he was in his combat gear, which he wore whenever he was on duty guarding Taevas. She hungered to see all that gorgeous skin, every slab of thick muscle. She loved that in the day his skin was that deep, beautiful green and at night a purple so dark, it looked like he was swathed in starless night sky. She wanted to run her fingers over every inch.

Her research had named this feeling as *attraction*. Lust. Touch-hunger. She wanted to *feel* Vael in a way she wanted to feel no one else.

She bubbled with the need to be near him. Anticipation made her hair stand up around her in a snapping, sizzling cloud of electricity. Hele took a step forward, pebbles shifting under her bare soles, and opened her mouth to tell him what she had decided.

"Hele, what in the gods names are you doing out here by yourself?" Vael's voice was tight, his brows lowered over glittering green eyes.

Her step stuttered. Instead of stopping with her usual quick, liquid grace, she stumbled on the stones. Surprise made her blink when she asked, "I... what? I was wandering."

Vael's lips, lush and soft-looking, pressed into a thin line. "You usually wander with Alex or your parents. Why are you by yourself so late?"

She bristled. It rubbed against her grain, the assumption that she needed her family to coddle her. Somewhere deep in her subconscious, she knew that it was *vital* her Chosen not see her as someone to be swaddled, but as the independent, powerful being she knew herself to be.

"I don't need a babysitter," she argued, chin jutting.

Vael cut his eyes away from her as he scrubbed a hand over his mouth. "No, you don't. You're not a baby. But you still shouldn't fly by yourself yet. What if something happened to you?" Was it her imagination, or did his expression tense when he said that? *Gods, I wish I could understand faces better.*

His wings flexed outward, huge and semi-translucent where the membrane stretched tight between bones, before they snapped back into a tight bundle against his armored spine. Her dragon made that chuffing sound again before his eyes swung back to her. They stayed studiously on her face, never dipping below her chin. More gently, he rumbled, *"Täht,* you should fly back to the nest. Your parents will worry if you are gone too long."

Her annoyance slid away, replaced by a swell of warm pride. Throwing her shoulders back, she took another step closer to him and announced in her carefully enunciated speech, "They will not worry because I do not live in the nest anymore."

Vael tilted his head to one side. "What do you mean? Of course you live in the nest."

Impatient, she bounced on the balls of her feet, hopping closer. The distance between them shrank with every rolling step. "No, I don't! You've been gone, so you haven't heard the news yet. I moved out of the nest and into my own dwelling."

Chapter Five

She expected a lopsided grin, perhaps like the one she received when she passed her exams, or the first time they crossed paths on the street and he said, *"Look at you, täht. You are beautiful in the sun."*

Instead, she got only a blank look, then a dawning disapproval. "Why would you do this? Are you ready to live on your own? It's only been two years, *täht.*"

She normally loved it when he called her *täht.* It meant star, and whenever he said it, she remembered what it felt like when he pressed her cold cheek against his chest and whispered to her in the darkness of his folded wings, *"You're safe. I have you now, my fallen star."*

Now she did not like it very much at all. Did Vael not see her as capable? As a woman ready to live her life? It was one thing when her family coddled her, but she discovered it was very, very different when Vael did it.

Her excitement ebbed. "I am ready," she insisted. Hele swallowed hard. "I am ready for all kinds of new things."

Vael's frown intensified. The wind ruffled the short strands of his dark hair. They tended to spike up between his largest pair of horns, and she'd wondered what it might be like to run her fingers through that funny tuft.

"What kind of things?" His tone was neutral, but the way his wings flexed seemed agitated. That was one emotion she could read well, since she felt it so often in the early days.

Taking a deep breath, Hele clapped her hands in front of her. "Well... Taevas asked me to consult with some witches studying m-weather. I'll be paid for my time, so one new thing is having a *job.*"

And didn't that tickle her! Not only would she be learning something new, but she would have responsibility, a *job,* just like everyone else she knew. Being a contained force of nature with no purpose wasn't healthy, she'd learned, so it was a relief to have even temporary work to do.

A bit of the tightness left Vael's expression. "That sounds wonderful, *täht.* I know how much you love learning, so R&D is the perfect place for you. Are you working with the people on loan from the Collective?"

A little bit of her ire was soothed by his easy support. Hele inched closer. If he noticed that they were only an arm's length away from each other now, he didn't show it. His eyes remained locked on hers.

Out of the corner of her eye, she caught the quick flicking of his tail and wondered what might cause it to do that.

Clasping her hands to her chest, she answered, "Yes. They're working on the r-siphon and they want to talk to me about it. I am very excited!"

There was the smile she longed for. "Fantastic." One hand lifted, as if he meant to reach out and touch her, before it fell back to his side. Crossing his arms over his chest, he asked, "And you're *really* okay with living on your own?"

Hele rolled her eyes. "*Yes.* I like it."

"Where is it? Near your parents?"

"No, it's in De Tour." She leaned closer, until her hair fell over her shoulders to ripple against her chest. This close, she could smell that spicy scent she dreamed of and even feel his delicious body heat. Sparks flew. "I have so many *neighbors!*"

His smile dimmed. "Do you feel safe there?"

"Of course I feel safe." She gave him a baffled look. "I can take care of myself."

"You can, but I worry." His expression turned wry. She was surprised to see his throat bob with swallow before he uncrossed his arms and slowly closed the distance between them. His palm, scaldingly warm against her cooler skin, cupped her cheek. In a rough voice, he whispered, "Feels like just yesterday you fell into my arms, *täht.*"

Hele's breath caught. She leaned into his touch without thinking as a coil of unfamiliar heat tightened in her belly.

Gods, is this what it's like to crave a touch?

She thought she understood the longing one felt for a mate, but when he touched her like that, when he *looked* at her like that, Hele felt like she was standing on the cusp of something so breathtakingly deep that it defied comprehension.

Vael's brows pinched. His wings spread slightly as he swayed forward, head dipping to stare into her eyes. "Why do you look like that? What did I do?"

She had no idea what her expression said because she did not understand her feelings herself. Instead of attempting to explain the massive thing expanding in her chest, she simply said, "I want to Choose you."

Those soft lips parted. The hand on her cheek flexed hard before it loosened again. In a voice like crushed gravel, he asked, "...what did you say?"

"I *Choose* you." Hele stretched up onto her tiptoes to press a featherlight kiss to the tip of his wide nose. Her dragon nearly went cross-eyed as he tried to follow the movement. "You will be my mate."

She expected him to pull her close like she had seen other dragons do — Constantin and Valerie were constantly tugging at one another, and the other couples she'd seen usually *at least* twined their tails when out and about. She did not have a tail, but her hair was quite long, and when she imagined him twining it around his green fist, something dark and sweet pooled in her belly.

This was what she had longed for, what she'd craved when she watched others. Mates were constantly petting and embracing, leaning down to whisper in each other's ears and kiss lips. So she waited, breath stuck in her throat, for her dragon to bring her closer.

Would he kiss her? She'd done all the research on that. Of course, she had learned that *reading* about something didn't always mean she could apply the knowledge well, but—

Vael's thumb, calloused and warm, skated across her cheek before he dropped his hand. Taking one precisely measured step back, he said, "*Täht... no.*"

Hele swayed, left off balance by his sudden movement. Confusion made her normally quick mind slow. "No?"

Though his expression was shadowed in the darkness, she still saw regret and... *Gods, that cannot be pity.*

"I'm sorry, Hele," he grated, voice raw. "But you can't Choose me. You aren't ready."

She had the unfortunate experience of emotional pain several times since her fall. Sometimes when she did something wrong in front of others, she felt humiliation. Sometimes a passing comment wounded her. Sometimes she lashed out and felt the ugly slush of guilt in her gut. Once or twice she had even cried and considered disappearing into the sky, where confusion and hurt and anger could not reach her so easily.

But *this...* This was a blow unlike any other.

Emotion came in awful flashes. First there was disbelief, then humiliation, and finally a screaming wall of pure, terrible *hurt.*

In a small, confused voice, she asked, "You... will not let me Choose you? I do not understand. You won't Choose me?"

Vael's expression was pained, almost *agonized,* when he choked out, "No."

"You do not want to be my mate." It wasn't a question this time, but rather a flat statement of fact like the others she sometimes recited to herself. *The 'Riik is my home. My clan is Aždaja. My name is Hele Aždaja, daughter of Constantin and Valerie. My Chosen does not want me.*

"I... Hele, that's not—" He reached for her again, but this time her body moved on instinct. She bounded backward. In an instant, there were several feet between them. She wished it were more. She wished she had never gone wandering. She wished she'd never said anything to him at all.

"I don't understand," she croaked, looking everywhere but him. All the signs were there. He'd embraced her. He gave her gifts — *blankets* for her nest! That is what mates did. She knew this. She'd observed it and she'd read about it. Dragons only gifted nesting material to their Chosen, so that they might make a roost together. She'd done her research, assembled the evidence, and come to the only conclusion that made sense.

But he didn't want her as his mate. Why? Did she do something wrong? Was it because she wasn't a dragon like Alex, strong and sensual and confident? Did he find her stilted speech offputting?

Hele was horrified by a possibility she'd never considered before. *Is he not attracted to me? Does he want another?*

Jealousy, as brittle and hard as hail, pelted her. On the heels of that came the equally terrible thought, *Of course he would have another. What are you? A naive elemental who just learned her letters, who thinks that having her own nest makes her special. He's part of your Isand's Wing. Important. Powerful. I am nothing to him. Nothing but a helpless creature following his shadow from below.*

Vael stepped toward her, his wings extended to their full width. "*Täht*, listen to me. I only want—"

Hele balked. "I will *not* hear what you want!" She couldn't bear it. She could not hear a name. She could not know who she would be comparing herself to for all her days. Her heart, tender and new, could not take it.

Thunder clapped overhead, so close it shook the ground. Water whipped up until the spray reached them even as far as they were from the churning waves. Deep in the roiling clouds, lightning streaked in angry slashes.

The light briefly illuminated her dragon's stricken expression, but Hele was not moved by it. Her mate did not want her. Her mate wanted someone else. She thought the fall had been the most terrifying, painful moment of her life, but his rejection took its place with ease. At least the fall was something she could recover from.

This? She did not think she would ever heal from this.

Despite the lightning and the wind that had begun to claw at their bodies, Vael crossed the distance between them. He was a huge, hulking shape in the dark. Clawed hands grasped her shoulders and the massive shapes of his wings began to close around her, shielding her from the storm she created.

"My Hele, *no,*" he rasped, barely audible over the howling wind.

No, I will not be your mate. No, I will not Choose you.

Fine then, she thought, jerking her shoulders out from under his hands. She could not bear his touch. It made her *feel* and all those feelings for him needed to be carved out with claw and fang. *If he will not be my mate, then I will find someone else to Choose me!*

Sucking in deep, shuddering breaths, she raggedly informed him, "I do not want you to pity me. I do not want you to take care of me." She looked at the wings that were halfway encircled around her and cried, "You do *not* get to embrace me! Only my mate will do that!"

She knew that she would regret being angry with him tomorrow, when the pain began to dull, but she did not care. Perhaps she would apologize. Perhaps not.

Maybe I will avoid him for the rest of my life.

Yes, that sounded good. If she never had to look at him again, she would not feel this awful longing and its accompanying rejection. It was irrational, but it was the only solution she could think of in the moment.

"I'm sorry," he replied. Desperation made his expression contort as rain began to slide down his forehead, his cheeks, his chin. "I'm sorry, Hele. This isn't how I wanted to have this conversation. Please just listen—"

But she did not *want* to listen, just as he did not *want* her.

Hele, who was once vast and powerful and incomprehensibly old, was reduced to something small, and lonely, and pitied by the man she wanted above all others.

It was fucking *galling*.

Lightning snapped overhead. Vael's head jerked up as his arms moved to circle her, perhaps to shield her from the strike, but he only stumbled, his wings and arms folding over nothing but hot air.

Chapter Six

Vael stumbled into his dwelling blindly. "Fucking *fuck!*"

Hele's storm raged outside. Every savage blast of wind, every icy raindrop, and every clap of thunder felt like a recrimination. He was soaked to the bone beneath his armor. He was also absolutely heartsick.

Gods, what have I done?

Lights came on automatically as he dragged his booted feet across the threshold of the glass door and into the anteroom. His home, built of sturdy, sigil-reinforced stone and metal, shook with the force of the storm.

Vael stumbled through the large, empty room and into the living area, where a sunken couch and comfortable cushions held pride of place — ready for guests he never had and a mate he'd just savaged.

He looked for her, of course. Even when the storm threatened to shred his wings, he'd scoured the sky for her, desperate to find his Hele and explain—

Explain what? Explain that I'm still fucking rejecting her?

He knew he was doing the right thing. She was still too young, no matter what she said, to commit to something like matehood. She needed more time. More life. More room to stretch her wings. He couldn't cage her without sewing regret, and if there was one thing he could never accept, it was that Hele might someday wish she hadn't Chosen him. She needed time.

He *knew* that.

Because once she was his, he wasn't letting her go. He was going to sink his claws into her soul and hold on until the day Grim dragged him to the Underworld. Vael would demand everything of her — every bit of her heart, every bit of her joy, every bit of her body — and he would give himself over completely in exchange.

There was no fucking way she was ready for that level of commitment yet. As far as he knew, she hadn't shown so much as a flicker of romantic or sexual interest in anyone. What did she know of Choosing? Of relationships? Perhaps his wickedly intelligent mate read about both subjects, but she didn't *know* what they meant. Not really.

She couldn't know that when she Chose him, it took every bit of willpower he possessed to keep from crushing his mouth to hers, bearing her down onto the rocks, spreading her legs, and claiming her right there on the beach for all to see. As far as he was aware, she did not feel lust or touch-hunger like he did.

She couldn't know that he wanted to hear every thought that zipped through her mind, or that he worried about her constantly. Did she even understand what it meant to be so consumed by someone that your day began and ended with them? Did she consider that if one day she decided matehood was not what she wanted, he would shatter?

Hele could not know that when he thought of stifling her, locking her into a relationship she didn't want, he felt sick to his stomach.

He could not, *would not* clip her wings.

Unfortunately, he also knew that explaining his position would not do a damn thing to help or soothe her. In her place, it certainly wouldn't have made a difference to him.

But he had to fix things. There had to be a way to make her understand. He never meant to reject *her,* just the timing. It was too soon. But he'd been so shocked by her announcement — shocked and honored and disbelieving and overjoyed — that the only word he could get out was *no.*

It took him too long to register what she said because he'd been struggling with the temptation to kiss her. They were so close. He could feel the cool, silken skin beneath his palm and the tiny, thrilling bite of her lightning. His rigid control over his impulses had worn down into dust as he watched her lips part.

Just one kiss, he'd thought, desperate. *Just one. Just something to hold onto for a while longer.*

And then he swayed forward, his heart pounding, only to be stopped short by her innocent declaration.

She Chose me.

"Stupid— *fucking!* Gah!" He tore at his armor until the latches on his shoulders and side gave way. Tossing his vest carelessly onto the floor, he quickly sent his arm and leg plates to join it. Standing in his soaked black fatigues, he ran a shaking hand through his hair and tried to *think.*

You can fix this. You can. Gotta track her down and make her listen. That's step one.

His head was still spinning from the news that she was no longer in her family's dwelling. His concern had been quickly supplanted by her declaration, but as soon as he recalled that he had no idea where she lived now, he felt his wings snap out with barely suppressed agitation.

The scars from the war had long since faded under skillful healing hands, but the intricate nerves in the paper thin membrane between the bones had never quite recovered. That meant he had slightly less control over his wing movement than most dragons, and that tended to manifest most strongly in moments of stress.

It was *also* why he struggled to keep from wrapping them around his Hele. It was an automatic response to her nearness, and one he had to consciously keep in check whenever she came within a few feet of him.

He would have done anything to have her in his embrace just then. Anything.

Hele might still be out on her own right now. Or she could be at her new home, upset and hurting and alone while I'm here being fucking useless.

But he wasn't useless. He was a member of the Isand's Wing, and he was a seasoned soldier. He knew how to solve a problem under pressure.

Forcing his wings to fold against his back, he tried to organize his thoughts into an actionable list. *First, find out where her dwelling is. Second, apologize. Third...*

His mind went blank. What was there to do after that? He wanted to say they'd go back to normal, but was there a normal after this? *Worry about that later.*

Vael raised his fingers to his jaw, ready to activate the biomechanical implant that worked as a communication device, but the faint beeping in his ear beat him to it. A small flare of magic and a touch answered the call. He held his breath, irrationally hoping that it would be Hele's voice on the other end of the line.

It wasn't.

"You're going to give me one very good reason why I shouldn't tear the wings from your back."

Vael's heart dropped. "Artem, now is not the fucking time."

"I bet it isn't." Artem, Hele's adopted older brother and Taevas's cousin, normally had a charming, almost lackadaisical personality that hid a cunning and decisive mind. All that usual good cheer was completely stripped away. There was nothing but pure menace when he growled, "You know how I know that, Vael? I just got a call from Alex, who has spent the last two hours trying to console our sister."

Two hours? *Two hours.* A vice tightened around Vael's throat. He croaked, "Is she all right?"

Artem was pitiless. "No, she's not all right. You made my

sister cry, you jackass. She won't say what happened and Alex is worried you did something to her. She's about five seconds away from hunting you down and skinning you alive. I *know* you'd never touch my sister, so what the fuck did you say to Hele?"

Vael stared bleakly into the hallway that led to his cold nest. It was his pride and joy, draped in tapestries he'd collected over his long life and absolutely filled to the brim with cushions and blankets. Every scrap of fabric was either pale blue, green, or violet — the colors that looked prettiest against Hele's opalescent skin. He knew she didn't sleep, so he'd installed special low watt reading lights and bookshelves in the walls. That way his mate could indulge in her favorite pastime while he held her all night.

He hadn't slept in there once since he bought the roost. He couldn't bear to.

"She Chose me," he answered, hollow. "She just... I was flying in to check on her. She was out by herself, so I landed and we talked and— she just *did it.*"

There was a cold, stunned silence for several heartbeats before Artem asked, "And what did you say, Vael?"

"I told her no, of course." Gods, the words felt like gravel when they came out.

"You told her *no.*"

Vael scrubbed at his wet face with his palms, suddenly angry. "Yes! I told her no!"

"Why the fuck did you *do* that?"

"What do you mean, *why?*" He let out a short, furious shout to the ceiling. Did no one care about her? Did no one see the danger of her being stifled so soon, when she was just finding her wings? Vael felt like he was losing his damn mind. "She's not *ready!*"

"...Do you mean to tell me that my little sister, the woman you've been pining after since the moment she dropped from the sky, told you she wants to be your mate and you— you said *no?*"

The flat incredulity in Artem's voice was almost as unendurable as his own hideous guilt. Vael propped his hands on his hips and hung his head. After taking several deep breaths, he gritted out, "You know why."

Artem didn't miss a beat. "Yeah, you're a dumb motherfucker."

A hot flush washed over the back of his neck. He'd known Artem since he was a baby. They'd flown together often, and being a few decades his senior, Vael had enjoyed watching him go from mischievous little boy to proud soldier. What he did *not* enjoy was being called out by a dragon both younger than him and below him in rank. Usually it would have rolled off his back, but not at that moment, when he already felt like he was being torn apart.

Voice sharpening, he barked, "Listen, you don't understand because you haven't been here. You don't—"

"You finish that sentence and I'm going to *actually* beat the shit out of you. Don't you dare say that I don't know my sister."

Vael winced. The indignation bled out of him in an instant.

He'd overstepped and he knew it. With his instincts in a tangle, it was easy to let the possessiveness twist things in his mind, to make him believe that he was the only one who *really* knew Hele. While it was true that he had spent more time with her in person than Artem had, seeing as the younger dragon had a mate and a child on the way across the country, he knew that he took his responsibilities as a brother seriously. Hele told him how they did family board game nights, and how Paloma and Artem wanted her to visit after the baby was born.

"I think I'll wait a few months," she'd admitted to him, her aquiline features drawn with worry. *"I don't want to accidentally shock a newborn."*

His Hele. Always so considerate and painfully aware of her differences. Gods, he loved her.

But Artem loved her, too. To imply otherwise was not just offensive, it was shameful. They were clanmates, for godssakes.

Vael rubbed his stinging eyes. "I'm sorry."

"I'm not the one you should be apologizing to."

"I *know,* but I don't know where— wait." He straightened and narrowed his eyes. Sharply honed hunting instincts prowled to the forefront of his mind. "You know where her apartment is, don't you?"

A huffed breath came across the line. "Sure do."

"Tell me."

"No."

Vael's tail began to whip behind him in quick, agitated strokes. "Why the fuck not? I need to fix things, Artem. And you know it fucking kills me to not know where she is right now. You *know.* If it was your mate, what would you do? How would you feel right now?"

"Actually, seeing as she's very much not your mate, I don't think you have any right to know where her new dwelling is."

Now *that* was too fucking far. Vael snarled, *"She is my mate!"*

"Sure doesn't sound like it to me."

"Why are you doing this? Don't you want me to fix it?"

"No," Artem answered, voice dropping into a low, threatening cadence. "What I want you to do is make up your fucking mind. Either you want her to be your mate or you don't. It's that simple, Vael. You don't fuck around with someone like this. You especially don't fuck around with my sister."

Before he could defend himself, Artem continued, "So the way I see it, you have two options: either crawl on your knees and beg her to take you, or you leave my sister alone. For good. No more gifts. No more trips to the library. No more messages. You get out of her life so she can let you go. Let her find someone else."

He felt the breath leave him in one great *whoosh.* Let her find someone else? The part of him that was more beast than man roared with furious denial.

Over his godsdamned corpse!

The idea of leaving her was so entirely unacceptable it could not be considered. She was his true north. His fallen star. *His.* Without her, his life was quiet, and dull, and cold. Without her he had no nest and no warmth. He couldn't even imagine it. He *refused*.

But that didn't mean she was anymore ready for matehood than she was yesterday. Just because *he* couldn't live without her, didn't mean that he should force her into something she wasn't ready for. That was the part that Artem just didn't get. He wasn't the one who caught her. He wasn't the one who held her as her body spasmed, as she fought to communicate. He didn't know how much she deserved to *live*.

He didn't know that Vael saw his own pain in her struggles. Artem was born long after the war, and likely had no idea that Vael, now the highest rank a dragon could achieve in the 'Riik's military besides *Isand*, was once a lost, voiceless creature. He did not know what it was like to have your wings clipped and your choices stolen.

But Vael wasn't a verbose man. He struggled to articulate his thoughts even when he wasn't being choked by raw emotion. So he simply replied, "I can't let her go. You know I can't. I won't."

"Then I guess you'd better start crawling, asshole."

Chapter Seven

The next day, Hele tucked another important life milestone under her metaphorical belt: after spending an entire night crying into her nest with her outraged sister there for moral support, she'd peeled herself out of the blankets, threw on a dress, and forced herself to go to work.

Any excitement she had for her appointment with the witchy duo on loan from the Coven Collective had popped like a balloon. While she rode the m-lev to Mackinaw City, where the western research hub of the 'Riik government was located, she tried to untangle exactly what she felt. While the night before had been crushing disappointment, hurt, and confusion, this morning she just felt... worn out.

Hele of the boundless energy and curiosity had been utterly deflated by Vael's rejection.

What do I do now? She had so many grand plans for her life. All of them involved her own personal sun, her big green dragon, and now...

Now she was cut loose, drifting in a way that was distinctly uncomfortable.

Alex told her that heartbreak came in waves. Sometimes it crashed over you, and sometimes it rose slowly, almost unnoticed, until it closed over your head and stole your breath. Though she did not know how to swim, Hele thought she was already under water.

She did not even begin to surface until she was sitting in a nondescript office, her hands folded in front of her and her head turned to look out the window at the rolling waves of Lake Michigan, white-tipped and hypnotic.

I am Hele Aždaja. I live in the Draakonriik. I have my own dwelling. I am angry, she thought dully. *And I am sad.*

"Hele?"

She turned. A woman with a head of thick ringlets stood in the doorway. She was buxom, with generous curves and a round, smiling face. Her skin was what her mother called *"peaches and cream"* and her eyes were twin circles of vivid blue. There was something *different* about her, though Hele didn't have the vocabulary to put a finger on what exactly it was. Perhaps it was the keen look in her eyes, a cunning sort of air that made the hair on the back of her neck stand up.

A witch, her mind supplied. *That's what's different. There's some strange magic in her.*

Standing up from her seat, Hele smoothed her palms down the front of her flowy dress. Static crackled in their wake. "Yes. I'm Hele Aždaja."

"Oh, lovely! I'm Ruby. Ruby Goode." The woman stepped inside, allowing someone else to slip in and close the door behind her. There was a flutter of long brown hair and the crackle of magic as the door swung shut without a touch. Ruby gestured to her companion. "This is my research partner, Atria Le Roy."

Atria looked more like Hele in body type, though there were of course, massive differences between them. While they were both lean, Atria was bronze-skinned, with waves of mahogany hair that fell to her waist. Her hips were generous, and her features were almost catlike in their elegance.

Most curious were the tattoos on her wrists: two shackles of vivid red ink rendered in stark, circular designs like cuffs.

Hele tilted her head to one side. A little bit of her malaise cleared, burned away by curiosity. She recognized those markings from her extensive reading on the gods. Only one order boasted tattoos like that. *Burden's Bonded.* A secretive hereditary priestesshood and one of the last in the world. "You are a priestess?"

Atria's smile was smaller than Ruby's, more reserved. There was a tightness around her eyes when she answered, "In a past life I was, yes."

"I've never met a priestess before." She paused, thinking. "Even a retired one."

Her smile widened. "I've never met an elemental before, so it looks like we're even."

Hele brushed her long white hair over her shoulder and preened, just a little. She looked at them through her lashes. A little bit more of her heartbreak fell to the wayside, momentarily dulled. "Maybe not. Elementals are more rare than priestesses, I think."

Ruby guffawed. "That is absolutely true! You wouldn't believe the trouble we've had getting in touch with elementals for this project."

"Trouble?" Hele blinked. "Calamity doesn't seem very hard to find."

"He doesn't do interviews," Atria explained, sliding gracefully into the office chair facing the window.

Ruby sank into a chair as well. Her smile hadn't dimmed even a little bit. It was what her father would have called *megawatt.* "Most elementals won't even give us a chance to say hello, let alone sit down and talk for a while."

Hele considered this as she returned to her seat. Her long, gauzy skirt flowed over her legs as she settled. Slowly, she replied, "I... do not think that we like to be known by strangers. It's exposing."

Atria threaded her long fingers together on the tabletop and pressed, "Exposing?"

"I don't know if that is the right word," she answered,

annoyed and self-conscious of her limited vocabulary. Unbidden, Vael came to mind. *Is this one of the reasons he will not have me? Because I struggle sometimes?* If that was the case, then she knew he did not deserve her.

It still hurt, though, to think that perhaps he did not think her fit to be Chosen because she didn't know all the words she wished to. It hurt a *lot.*

But maybe it's not how you speak, she thought, strangely compelled to make the bruised feeling in her chest worse. *Maybe it's because he wants someone else. A pretty dragon with wings and a tail to twine his with.*

Hele bit her lip to keep it from wobbling. *Stupid. I am an elemental. I am Aždaja. If he wants a dragon, then he is welcome to one. I will find someone else to Choose. Maybe another one like me.*

She cleared her throat of the lump that had formed there. Trying to be casual, she asked, "Have you met many others? I understand they don't want to speak with you, but maybe you know of them?"

A strange feeling of awareness made goosebumps prickle all over her body as Atria studied her. "We've tracked down a few. Calamity is the most famous, of course, but there are a handful of notable elementals that we were able to get a hold of."

Hele stared wistfully at her clasped hands. They looked strange to her — clawless, pale, faintly glowing with blue and purple and yellow light. No dragon skin, no pigment shift. Just *her.*

In a quiet voice, she said, "I would like to meet one of mine someday. It is good being dragonkin, but... I would like to know others." *Maybe one of mine would Choose me.*

It would be a good thing, if Vael did not want her, so why did the thought make her want to cry again?

Ruby's expression softened. "Well, of the few elementals I've been privileged enough to meet in our research, you are the only one who has chosen to live amongst a large population. The general consensus is that elementals are solitary. It makes sense, frustrating as it can be for us, that your people would not want to sit down and be interviewed by strangers. You might have better luck, though."

Yes, that was the conclusion Hele had drawn as well. Her reading backed it up, but so did her own instincts. How often had she found herself over stimulated, craving the vastness of before? It was lonely and she had the vague sense that she'd hated it, but it was also... peaceful. Secure. Still.

I felt still again when I was with Vael. Like she was floating, but not so far away as to lose everything she loved. A perfect stillness. Quiet but not lonely. Free but loved.

Perhaps she was meant to be solitary, but she did not think it was a rule. She did not *want* to be solitary. She was part of a clan, and that meant she was part of something bigger than herself. It was a privilege very few were offered.

"Most of my people are not dragonkin. They do not know how to adapt. I learned." Her gaze darted between the two women. She would think on her kind more later, when she was alone.

Changing the subject, she announced, "I want to help my clan. And you. Maybe after I do this, I will help mine, too."

Atria's lips curved to form another warm smile. Her eyes were soft. Hele struggled to come up with something to compare them to. The best she could summon was the wood of Taevas's throne — warm and polished silky smooth, but tough enough to last centuries surrounded by dragonfire.

Her voice was gentle but firm, too, when she said, "We are so, so grateful, Hele. Really, you can't imagine how excited we are to get this chance to speak with you."

"My Isand said you are working on the r-siphon project." She wrinkled her nose. "He said he renamed it *Project Lightning Bolt.*"

Ruby waved her hand in the air in a *half this, half that* gesture. "Yes and no. We consulted on it early on, and have used a lot of the research in our work, but we have spent the past ten years on a clean energy project for the United Congress."

That took her by surprise. After a brief consultation with her internal word filing system, she asked, "Clean energy? What does that have to do with elementals?"

Ruby's eyes, cunning and beautiful, glittered in the sunlight. *"Everything."*

～

They emerged from the meeting room two hours later. Ruby was muttering quietly to herself, her phone in her hand and her thumbs flying across the screen in a blur. She walked briskly down the hall without waiting to see if anyone would follow her.

Hele, mentally exhausted but full to the brim with academic excitement, drifted toward the elevator bank that would take her back down to the ground level. Her hair was a trail of sparks behind her. By her side, Atria walked with her hands tucked loosely behind her back, hidden by the folds of her ankle-length skirt. Every step revealed flashes of dark bronze skin behind the slit that ran down from her thigh.

They stopped at the elevator. A moment after Hele pressed the button, Atria quietly cleared her throat. "It was wonderful talking with you today. I look forward to picking your brain some more."

Hele couldn't quite suppress a grin. "I liked speaking to you. I want to know everything about your project. About your science."

Atria made an inquisitive noise in the back of her throat and shifted her stance until she was leaning over slightly, toward Hele. Her warm brown eyes were laser focused when she asked, "Have you passed your basic education assessment yet?"

"Yes."

She hadn't known how competitive she was until she learned what *scores* and *exams* and *grades* were. When she learned that passing the BEA with high scores was the way to open up more education, she'd thrown every ounce of her being behind acing the tests. Her results had come in just the month previous. When she opened the email, her family had nearly burst her eardrums with their roars of joy.

"If you don't mind me asking, what were your scores?"

Hele sent her a sharp smile. "All five hundreds except for math. I am not as good with numbers. My sister Paloma had to tutor me, but I still did not do as well as I wanted. I got four-seventy."

Atria reeled backward, her expression loosened with surprise. "That's *incredible*, Hele."

"My *ema* calls me a genius," she replied, shrugging. "I do not think this is right. I am just *very* determined." Another smile, sly this time. "And I do not need to stop reading to sleep. My *isa* calls that a tactical advantage."

"Genius or not, you're damn smart, Hele. I think you would do really well in science. If you're interested, Ruby and I know a lot of people in the Collective. There are tons of programs that you could look into."

She turned her head so fast, the ends of her hair slapped against the elevator door. Sparks sailed through the air to burn tiny holes in the thin carpet under their feet. "What?"

Atria shrugged, but her gaze was intent on Hele's face when she replied, "It's just a thought. Those kinds of scores, a recommendation, and your natural enthusiasm can get you almost anywhere. I started with a lot less than that, and I still somehow managed it. You could enter just about any university you wanted in the Collective."

Suddenly overwhelmed, Hele turned to face the chrome elevator doors again. Her mind raced. *Leave the 'Riik? Go to school? Become a scientist? No, I can't do that. I can't leave because my mate is—*

But she did not have a mate, and her family could fly to see her anywhere. Being Aždaja did not begin, nor end, at the 'Riik's borders. It was a forever thing. Theoretically, she could go anywhere, do *anything*.

It was an offer of freedom that should have thrilled her wild heart, but instead it just made the bruising worse.

"I— I will think on this," she promised, blinking back a frustrating prickle of tears.

"You don't have to answer now. It's a standing offer." The elevator dinged and the doors began to slowly slide open, but she didn't take a step before Atria pressed just the tips of her fingers against her bare arm.

Hele turned to stare at the witch, surprised that she would risk it when most non-dragons feared the constant pulses of energy that made her skin flicker. It was harmless, but it was also different, and Hele understood that differences were often threatening.

She'd even wondered if perhaps that was why Vael had stopped touching her after those first few days. Did he worry she would hurt him? Or did he simply... not like her skin?

The insecurity was buried under dense layers of Aždaja pride, but it was there all the same. A crack in an otherwise strong foundation.

Her throat constricted painfully. That small, tentative touch from the witch meant the world to Hele.

Atria's lovely face, heart-shaped and expressive, was wreathed in concern. Speaking quickly, she said, "I know this is forward, but it's hard for me to— I'm... sorry you're hurting. If you'd like to talk, you can call me any time. I may not be able to understand what you're going through, but I can listen, and if you'd like help, I can soothe some of the pain."

Hele stared. "What— How do you know?"

"I'm an empath." Atria dropped her hand. She carefully tucked both behind her back once more when she ruefully added, "Not much use in science, but in my other life, I helped the heartsick. I can do the same for you, if you'd let me."

Her heart lurched. She knew what empaths did. They helped blunt the worst of emotional pain, working skillfully to untangle deeply embedded psychological wounds and amplify positive feelings through the exchange of energy. For a wild moment, she almost jumped at the chance to put distance between herself and all the ugly new feelings.

She could make the heartbreak and doubt disappear.

It was so tempting, but when Hele opened her mouth to say yes, she couldn't force the word out.

A sharp stab of possessiveness held her tongue.

What would happen if she didn't feel this way? Would she not care about Vael anymore? Would he simply drift from her mind like a cloud on the horizon?

The feelings hurt, but they belonged to *her.* They should not be dulled, or stripped from her. Hele wished that she could cut out the part of her that loved Vael so that the pain would not be so great, but she was too selfish to ever truly consider it. Her feelings for Vael belonged to her and to her alone. What she did with them was no one's business — not even his.

And though he did not want her in the way she wanted him, Hele refused to give him up entirely.

"Thank you," she whispered, wrapping her arms around herself. Her chest felt bruised, but she did not think that was a bad thing. Not completely, anyway. "But some things, I think, are good for me to know. Even the bad things. I am... adapting."

Atria nodded. A small, sad smile curled her lush lips when she answered, "Yeah, I understand. Some things you just have to feel. But if you ever change your mind or you just want to talk, call me. We can discuss programs, too. Don't forget that."

Hugging herself tighter, Hele stepped into the elevator. "I will."

Maybe she wouldn't let the witch take her heartbreak, but her other offer didn't sound too bad at all.

If there is nothing keeping me here, then maybe it's time for me to wander.

CHAPTER EIGHT

IT TURNED OUT TO BE A GOOD THING THAT TAEVAS HAD
given him the week off. There was no way Vael could have focused
on his duties after a sleepless night of searching for Hele. She
hadn't answered any of his calls or messages, so he'd pulled in
every favor he had to try and track her down. Unfortunately, no
one knew where her new apartment was — or rather, no one was
willing to tell him.

While a part of him was deeply relieved that no one had given
up the location of her dwelling purely from a safety and privacy
perspective, he was left pacing his living room all night, worried
sick about her.

At least Alex was with her, he thought as he forced himself
into a quick, cold shower. Water pelted the bunched muscles of
his shoulders and back. *But it should be me who soothes her when
she's hurt.*

If only he hadn't been the one to hurt her in the first place.

Around and around he went, agonizing over what he could
have said, how he could have handled her announcement better, if
only he weren't so shit with words. He was deeply embarrassed by
the way he reacted and desperate to smooth things over with her.

If only I knew where she was!

The only advantage he had was that he knew where she was supposed to be the next day: meeting with the witches on loan from the Collective.

He knew they weren't given full security clearance, so they would be confined to the publicly accessible research facility in Mackinaw. It was a short flight away. Not that it mattered. He would have crossed oceans to apologize to her.

Throwing on his usual jeans and a plain black t-shirt, both specially designed to accommodate his wings and tail, Vael threw himself off of his perch as soon as the sun crested the horizon. He didn't know when her appointment was, so he was determined to be there as soon as the doors opened, just in case.

As it happened, he still somehow missed her in the crush of bodies streaming in to work that morning. There were too many entrances to the huge, glass-walled building, and without knowing exactly where she was supposed to meet the witches, he could only circle the building restlessly, a hunter on the prowl.

It didn't do him a lick of good. Only the faint trace of her soft, clean scent by the main doors told him that she was *there*, but it still wasn't enough.

Hours passed. He posted up on a stone bench beneath a leafy tree, his elbows on his knees and his eyes glued to the doors. Of course he considered barging into the building to hunt her down, but being one of the Wing meant he had certain responsibilities: mainly not scaring the piss out of all the soft-skinned researchers inside.

His tail lashed back and forth behind him. *Hurry up, täht.*

Passersby gave him a wide berth. They might have anyway, seeing the circular tattoos on his arms, but his clear agitation didn't help things.

Dragons often affected an easy-going demeanor. They had a reputation for being territorial, acquisitive, and quick-tempered, so many of his kind went out of their way to hide their true nature until they got whatever it was that they wanted. Artem was great at that. Easy-going, charming. He hid his true nature under a veneer of aggressive affability, just as Taevas did.

But Vael was too old to hide and too frank to give a shit what anyone thought of him.

Besides Hele.

He was torn up with the need to fix what he'd accidentally broken, and he didn't care if he looked like he was a half-step away from lighting the whole godsdamned research facility on fire because of it.

Fire's not a bad idea, he thought, mulish and increasingly impatient. The longer he waited, the more he felt like a bomb about to explode. *If I set off the alarm, she'll have to—*

There. A flash of pale skin. The flutter of a long, lavender dress. The tell-tale glow. His Hele.

Vael shot up from his bench so fast, he scared a bird out of the tree behind him. He didn't notice its indignant squawk as he hopped over a hedge and jogged around people to catch up with her.

Gods, she's so pretty.

He loved to watch her walk. Hele just sort of... floated. Her hair moved on its own, sometimes reaching high with bursts of lightning through the strands, sometimes in a current around her back. Today it was down. The stillness was unusual, but it let him briefly admire just how long and silky the strands were when they swayed.

Her long, lean form moved fluidly. Her gait was almost unnaturally smooth, but she never seemed to notice when people stopped to look at her, their mouths open and eyes wide.

He noticed. Vael glowered at all the gawkers as he closed the distance between them. As soon as they made eye contact with him, they scattered like frightened little mice. *Not worthy of my Hele.*

She was just turning off the main path when he caught up to her.

"Hele!" He gently cupped her arm, stopping her. Her skin was so, so soft under his palm. "My Hele, please—"

She whirled around. Immediately, white hair fanned out around her, sparking and snapping with electricity. Without thinking, he mantled his wings, meeting her agitation with his own. The few people unwise enough to walk near them immediately swerved out of their way.

"Vael." Hele crossed her arms and took a deliberate step back. He was forced to let go of her arm, though he wanted nothing more than to pull her into the safety of his embrace. He wasn't good with words, but *touch...* He knew how to speak with his hands, his actions — if only she'd listen.

She glanced at his spread wings and scowled. Her tone was arch when she demanded, "What are you doing here? You should be on duty."

"I have the week off." He swallowed hard. Was the skin around her dark, fathomless eyes a little puffy? Did she look tired? Was her soft, floaty dress a little wrinkled, like she'd thrown it on without thinking this morning?

His heart gave a painful, guilty twist. *My poor Hele.*

"Good for you," she replied, already turning away. "Enjoy your vacation."

"Hele!" He lunged forward and spread his wings again, stopping her from stepping around him. "Please, I just want to talk to you. We left things badly last night and it's killing me."

She stopped abruptly and stared at him for the span of several heartbeats before she tightened her arms. Her black eyes shifted away from his face to study the ground. "There is nothing to talk about. You don't Choose me. Alex says that happens sometimes and I should move on."

He watched her elegant throat work for a moment as she found her words. Quietly, with raw feeling, she went on, "I know that it is— that I am not being fair when I get angry with you for it. But I am bruised, and I do not want to talk about it any more.

My feelings are mine. You do not get to know them, not when you do not *want* them."

Vael had been a soldier for over one hundred years. He'd been shot, stabbed, clawed, and imprisoned. He watched his small clan die when their roost was shelled in the final days of the war, and he'd spent months recovering in a ward, the delicate bones of his wings shattered almost beyond repair and his voice lost to smoke inhalation.

He *knew* pain.

This was a different sort of agony — and utterly unbearable. Knowing that he had hurt his Chosen when she had graced him with an honor unlike any other, and then hearing her *lock herself away from him...* Vael would have picked fucking disembowelment over that.

"I *do* want your feelings." He stepped closer and raised his wings so that they had a small amount of privacy, though he was careful not to embrace her — no matter how much he wanted to. Lowering his voice, he said, "I'm sorry, *täht,* but you didn't give me a chance to explain last night."

He watched her blink several times, but still, she would not look at him. "You don't have to explain." The skin around her mouth pulled taut. "I don't want to hear about how you Chose a dragon, or that you don't want me because I'm... me."

Vael balked. "Choose *another?*"

The words made sense on their own, but strung together they were impossible to understand.

"What are you talking about?" he demanded, speaking more sharply with her than he ever had before. Normally he tried to soften his hard edges around her, but couldn't manage it on top of everything else. "Tell me, *täht.* Explain."

Hele's eyes finally swung up to meet his gaze. They were two completely black pools. No whites. No irises or pupils. Pure, unbroken blackness that conveyed everything and nothing at all. "I thought that you wanted to Choose me, but you didn't. Why else would you say no? You must want someone else, or you think

I'm too strange." She shrugged once. It was a quick, jerky movement terribly at odds with her usual grace. "I am *different.*"

Vael reeled. His heart, already aching, twisted again. *I've wounded my mate.*

He knew how hard she tried to fit in, how she'd worked herself to exhaustion to learn their language, to understand their culture. He knew that she felt like an outsider sometimes. He also knew that she was self-conscious of the differences he loved so much.

To know that he'd clawed a sensitive part of her so clumsily was horrifying.

Vael lifted his hands, but stopped himself from taking her into his arms at the last moment. He *needed* to hold her. The pounding instinct to touch, to soothe, made his hands shake. And yet he did not embrace her. She told him not to, and he would not cross that line until she gave him permission again.

Instead, he fisted his hands by his thighs and grated, "I do *not* Choose anyone else."

Hele's eyes widened. Her soft mouth, so pretty and round like a little cushion, parted with surprise. "What? But you said—"

"I said that you could not Choose me *now.*"

She made a distinctly dragonish little growl of frustration. "I don't understand."

"*Täht,* I haven't Chosen anyone else. I don't *want* anyone else." His throat threatened to close around his next sentence, but he forced it out anyway. "I want you, my Hele. I have since the moment I caught you. You are mine."

He watched her expression clear. Wonder made her eyes round in her aquiline face. "You... want me?"

Do I want you? My gods, Hele, if I wanted you more, there'd be nothing left of me.

"Yes," he rasped, daring to lean closer. She stood still, allowing him into her space, as he slowly began to fold his wings around them. It wasn't quite an embrace, but if she gave the word...

"You *Choose* me?"

"Yes, *täht.*"

He hadn't really had a choice. The moment he felt her slight weight in his arms, the look she gave him when she opened her eyes... Vael wove his life with hers without hesitation or regret. It was as natural as flying home. He knew the way instinctively. He knew Hele just the same.

He watched her angular brows — white, with a faint undertone of purple just like her skin — bunch together as she tried to make sense of what he told her. "Then... then why did you say no to me?" Her gaze darted back and forth across his face, seeking answers. "I don't understand you."

Now comes the hard bit.

CHAPTER NINE

VAEL FELT SWEAT BEGIN TO GATHER UNDER THE LOOSE collar of his t-shirt. He could practically feel Artem's warning lingering over him like a dark cloud. But he couldn't do either of the options the younger dragon suggested.

Accepting her or leaving her to find another — both were impossible.

"My Hele..." he cautiously began as he tried to find the right words. "I didn't mean to reject you. I would never do that. You... you *honored* me." Vael wanted to touch her so badly, the urge *burned* him. Instead, he pressed his palm flat against his racing heart and continued, "You can't imagine how badly I want to be your mate. It's all I think about."

He had half hoped Hele might melt for him then. Perhaps if he told her how much he wanted her, she would forget his blunder and accept that things could not move forward yet. Maybe she would smile, and tell him he was forgiven, and even press her lips against his skin again.

But Hele was smart as a whip and wore a dragon's pride. She did not melt. She *burned.*

His mate narrowed her eyes and brusquely replied, "You said *no.* Tell me why."

Vael hesitated. He promised himself he would never lie to her, but he also knew that there was no way the truth would go over well. His Hele had a temper, and when she set her mind to something...

There was no helping it. All he could do was try to soften the blow. Clearing his throat, he said, "You are too... It's too soon. You aren't ready yet."

There was a beat of silence, then, "You don't think I'm ready for a mate."

He stifled a wince. "...Not yet."

The hair rose on the back of his neck a second before Hele quietly replied, "I am not a baby. I am *thousands*, Vael. Eons."

His heart sank. It didn't take a hundred years of combat experience to know he was walking ass-first into a firefight. "*Täht*, I know."

"Do you know?" Her lovely face, fine boned and angular, contorted into an expression of deep, furious hurt. "You say that you want me. You *Choose* me, but you don't think I know when I'm ready? Do you think I'm stupid, or just ignorant?"

He knew the conversation was spinning out of his control, but Vael was helpless to stop it. "Neither, Hele," he vehemently denied. "You're so much more intelligent than I am. You're the most incredible person I've ever met. I just want you to live your life before I ask everything of you. That's all."

A streak of white-hot lightning cracked the air between them, forcing him to take a short step away. Hele's hair lashed. The ends fizzled out into pure electricity as she shot back, "I want to live my life. *With. You.* That's why I Chose you!"

Gods, hearing the words on her lips, even when she was spitting mad, was a dream come true. His heart beat a hard rhythm in his chest, desperate to break free of its cage and reach her.

I Choose you too, my Hele, he wanted to cry. *That's why I'm* doing *this!*

With that thought in mind, Vael threw up his hands and dared to creep closer. He didn't care if she struck him with lightning a thousand times. It barely registered through his tough dragon skin, and even when it did, he'd grown to crave the feeling of her energy buzzing through his nerves. Dropping his voice to a soothing rumble, he assured her, "You are my Chosen. I will never want anyone else. Just you. When you're ready."

Hele reeled backward. Her mouth opened and then shut. Slowly, a horrible, pained expression crept over her face. One willowy arm slashed between them. "You do *not* Choose me. You Choose me *later*, when *you* are ready. This is not the same!"

He balked. "It's not about me! It's about—"

She gave the center of his chest one solid, accusatory poke. He felt the heat it gave off, and knew that if his clothing hadn't been fire-proof it would have left a smoking hole behind. "It *is*. You decided that I am not ready without asking. When I told you I was ready, you decided it wasn't true. *You.*"

Hele dropped her hand and leaned backward. Her gaze raked over him, hurt but full of fire. "I am Hele of Clan Aždaja. I was vast and powerful. I am *not* someone you Choose later, when you feel like it." Her narrow chin jutted forward. "I do not need to wait for you to decide on me. I can find a mate who is sure. Maybe one of my kind, or maybe a dragon, or even an elf. The only thing that matters is that they know who *I* am."

Vael could have taken her rejecting him for his mistake. He could have even understood if she simply didn't want him, surly and quiet and damaged as he was.

But he was not just a man. He was a dragon — a veteran of the Draakonriik's most elite unit, a warrior who had fought for his people, a boy who had lost everything once upon a time. He was quieter than many dragons, and he preferred a simple, isolated life, but he was still fiercely proud.

And possessive.

At the suggestion that she intended to find *another* mate even after Choosing him, Vael's restraint snapped like the delicate bone of a wing.

His shoulders thrust back and his head lifted. Standing military straight, he stared down his nose at his angry mate. His wings mantled again, two huge and threatening shapes tipped with five razor sharp talons. Vael would never harm a hair on her head, but another potential mate? Yes, he could do a tremendous amount of harm to *them*.

No one came between a dragon and their Chosen. No one.

In a hard, flat voice, he warned, "Do not test this, Hele. You have no idea the lengths I'll go to make you mine. You will not Choose someone else. *I* am your mate. *Me.*"

Hele's eyes glittered with challenge. "I'm sorry. I don't think I'm ready for that yet. Maybe later."

The air around her began to heat. Vael's lip lifted over his fangs with a warning snarl a second before he lunged. His arms locked around her lithe frame in a vice and his tail snapped around her slim leg, coiling tight. "Hele, do *not—*"

But it was impossible to hold her. He went temporarily blind as her form dematerialized in his arms. In the space between two heartbeats, she was gone.

"*Fuck!*" he bellowed, completely disregarding the wary looks of those few fools who still dared to share the street — if not the sidewalk — with him.

Vael stooped to snap up her discarded dress and dainty sandals. Clutching the messy bundle to his chest with one hand, he pointed a finger at the sky and announced, "Don't push me, *täht!* If you think I'm letting you go, you still haven't learned one fucking thing about dragons!"

The only response she offered was a single, sizzling strike to the tip of his claw.

～

A quick flight, a new dress, and a couple hours later, Hele met her sister for her lunch break as she'd promised the night before. Only

Alex ate anything, though. Hele spent the entire hour at the restaurant in the lavish shopping center on the bottom floor of the Roost giving her sister a furious play by play of her disastrous conversation with Vael.

Alex was utterly engrossed. She made a *pfft* sound when Hele got to the part where he said he wanted her, and then rolled her candy red eyes when she explained how he told her she wasn't ready. Her sister's reactions were big and loud, which was typical for every conversation with Alex. By the time they strode through the glass doors of the Public Relations department, where she was a junior assistant, *she* was the one ranting.

"Honestly, that *man*," she growled, leading the way to her desk, which sat just outside the head of the department's office. "Does he think that just because he pined after you for two years he has the right to tell *you* when you're ready? Typical pushy Wing bullshit. Those dragons always think they know better than everyone else. *Elite unit* this. *Look at my fancy tats* that. Completely insufferable. *Ugh.*"

Hele watched her sister's wings flex as she grabbed the back of her swivel chair and pulled it out from beneath her desk. Instead of a shirt, she wore an artfully arranged sash across her breasts, tied in a knot against her spine just below the base of her wings. Her wavy purple hair was cropped short into a cute pixie cut and her skin, a deep plum like their father's, shone with what the dragons called *liquid gold* — a glittery oil that kept their tough skin buttery soft. The glitter, Hele had learned, was purely for aesthetic purposes.

Overall, her sister was the complete opposite of Hele: vivacious, colorful, lushly figured, and problematically self-confident.

"He *pined* after me? What does this mean?"

Alex dropped into her seat and waved her clawed hand, decorated with several dainty gold rings, over the projected keyboard. The clear, razor thin screens strategically placed around her desk came awake with a pleasant chime.

"It means that he's had feelings for you forever and everyone knows it." Her lips pursed. "Well, except for you. But you had no reference, so..."

"But I *did* know!" Hele wanted to throw her arms up in frustration, but she knew that wasn't always a good idea when she was surrounded by delicate technology. Computers did not respond well to sudden movement, nor bursts of electricity. Very aware of the fact that she was one more smoking machine away from getting permanently banned from the PR department, Hele crossed her arms, muttering, "I knew it because he gave me blankets."

"Okay, fair. That was about as subtle as an m-lev. Your feelings, on the other hand, I never would have guessed. I thought you were totally oblivious. You've got a damn good poker face, Hele." Alex used her ID chip to log into the computer system. While she waited for everything to load, she leaned back in her chair and gave Hele an expectant look. "So... what're you gonna do?"

Aware that they were not alone, Hele lowered her voice when she answered, "I said that I would find a different mate."

Alex's expression didn't so much as flicker for several seconds before she slowly raised her eyebrows so high they almost touched her hairline. "Uh-huh? And how'd he take that?"

She shrugged. "I don't know. I didn't stay."

"*Ha!*" Alex slapped her thigh. A huge grin showed off her blindingly white teeth and popped the single dimple in her right cheek. "You dematerialized on his ass? Good. For. You. Always get the last word. That's the Aždaja way, baby. So good."

Was it, though? Hele didn't feel good about any of it. Fighting with Vael felt... wrong. But so did his high-handed assumption that *he* knew what was best for her.

That hurt almost as much as thinking he didn't want her.

Still, now that she knew he *did*... Hele wondered if she could truly follow through with her challenge. Truth be told, she had never felt any attraction toward another being aside from Vael — and she'd tried, just to be thorough. She felt nothing for the women, men, or the non-binary folk who crossed her path. It was only ever Vael she thought of, and it was only his touch she wanted.

But her pride had been torched, and that was not something to be borne.

"He doesn't think I'm ready for a mate," she said, anger and humiliation returning in a steady swell. "I think *he* is not ready. And if he isn't ready, that means he's not sure about me. I do not want someone who is unsure." Hele tugged on a lock of her errant hair, scowling. "One of the witches I met today said she would help me get into a program in the Collective. Maybe I should do it."

"Oh, sure." Alex waved a dismissive hand. "Every dragon has to go for a roam when they're young. If you want to go off and live in the Collective for a while, I don't see why you shouldn't. I've been thinking of roaming for a while, too." Her voice took on a softer note when she added, "Though I don't think you should do it just because of what's going on with Vael. You'd regret leaving things in a bad way. If you go, you should do it because you *want* to."

Alex cast her a sly look. "However, if you are thinking that it might be fun to find a mate, then I might be able to help you with that."

"I do not want to mate with any of your *lovers.*" That was what their mother called Alex's many besotted — and briefly entertained — paramours. Hele didn't get the full context of the joke, but she liked how it made their father roar with laughter whenever *Ema* said it.

"*People can't help themselves when faced with a dominant woman,*" he claimed, usually while giving his Chosen a sly look.

Hele was not dominant like Alex was. Perhaps that was why she struggled with Vael? Would he respect her choices more if she was the dominant one? She frowned even harder at the thought. *I do not think I am dominant or submissive. I am just me. I do not think I can change that now.*

Alex playfully swatted Hele's hip with her long, sinuous tail and rolled her eyes. "Please, I would never hook you up with one of my conquests. I don't keep their numbers, anyway. All I need to know is whether you want a dragon or not. Also gender, I guess, if you have a preference."

Hele considered this for several beats before she slowly answered, "Ah... male? But I do not think I want a dragon."

If she could not have *her* dragon, then she did not want one at all. And though she was dubious that anyone Alex might find would spark the same warmth in her that Vael did, she was also determined to try — if only so they *both* knew she was not the kind of woman who waited for someone to make up their mind.

"Easy-peasy." Alex popped her *p* with tangible relish. "I know just who to call."

"How do you know it will work?"

"Oh, I *don't* think it will work." Her sister swiveled toward her screens as the office began to fill up again, the allotted hour for lunch finally passed. "But I do think it will teach your dragon a good lesson about respecting your autonomy, and you might even learn something about yourself in the process." She shrugged, gilded shoulders moving in a graceful wave. "Hey, you may even like him! Worst case scenario, I know your date will be fine if he gets attacked by a jealous dragon."

Hele blinked.

She knew Vael was deadly. It was impossible to miss the way he moved in either form — like he was in perfect command of his body. He was roped with muscle and a tantalizing array of battle scars, not to mention the tattoos that swirled up and down both arms, marking him as one of the Wing. She'd seen him train with his comrades, so she knew he could fight with ruthless efficiency, but it was still impossible to imagine.

He had never been anything other than painfully gentle with her. In fact, he'd never even raised his voice around her until that afternoon. She struggled to imagine him attacking anyone, let alone because of *her*.

Still, curiosity made her ask, "Why would he be fine? Dragons are the strongest beings in the world."

Alex shot her a wink. "You're right, but elves are damn hard to kill."

CHAPTER TEN

"IF YOU'RE LOOKING FOR MY SISTER, SHE'S NOT HERE."

Vael scowled at the side of Alexandra's head. She was pretty, with dainty horns and dark purple skin that shimmered with gold, but she was also notoriously vicious. Calling on her was his last resort.

Artem's little sister casually shifted her purse to her other shoulder as she moved to wave her palm in front of the scanner by the octagonal glass door. The wind whipped off of the lake in sharp, biting gusts. If they didn't have dragon feet — a sort of semi-talon designed for gripping and take-off — they would have both been swept clean off of her perch by the force of it.

Raising his right wing high to shield his face from the worst of the wind, he growled, "You smell like Hele. I *know* you've been with her recently. Where is she, Alex?"

I am getting damn tired of asking that question. It felt like he'd done nothing but chase after his mate for the past twenty-four hours. He was so past *over it,* he had officially landed in *fucking done* territory.

Alex rolled her shoulders in an exaggerated shrug and Vael felt a vein in his temple begin to throb. Sweet as pie, she answered, "Hopefully having the time of her life right now."

Vael, already painfully tense, felt his hackles go up. "What does *that* mean?"

Alex stepped through the open door and into her apartment's anteroom. She didn't even spare him a glance as she shrugged off her purse and hung it on a hook. "It *means,* big bad dragon, that my sister is currently on a date with a *very* attractive elf and therefore *not available.*"

His mind blanked. Rebooted. Blanked again.

Hele is on a date with another man.

Of course, she warned him that she might seek a mate elsewhere, but he hadn't actually *believed* her. Vael's mind raced as he tried to think of who she might know, who she might go out with—

"Did you say an *elf?*" he snarled, storming into the anteroom with his tail rattling.

Alex wiggled her glittering fingers in the air. "Sure did!"

No.

His heart began to pound. Cold sweat dewed on the back of his neck. A tremor vibrated the delicate membrane of his wings. The echo of old terror made his stomach roll with nausea.

An elf. His breath shortened. *She's alone with an elf.*

He heard the whimpers of the dying and felt the awful dark closing in around him — one hour, then two, then a night, a day, and another, until a dark purple hand lifted the rubble to pull him free.

My Hele.

A dark sort of panic snaked around his throat and *pulled.*

His growl shook the frames on the walls. "She's with an *elf?* Elves are dangerous! What in the gods' names were you thinking?"

Alex whirled around, eyes flashing, and snapped her teeth an inch from his nose. Only his intensive training and experience kept him from snapping back. "*She* is dangerous, too! That is what you and my parents don't get! Hele can do whatever she pleases! If she wants to go out with an elf, then she will go out with an elf!"

He didn't often lose his temper, but there was no more restraint left in him. He felt any semblance of calm evaporate when he bit out, *"She. Chose. Me."*

Vael bared his fangs again. His wings spread in an intimidating display that would have made even fellow members of the Wing back down. Only Taevas, and perhaps poor, mad Radek would have gone toe to toe with him.

Alex belonged on that list, too, apparently. She spread her wings, her tail lashing, and spat back, *"You. Said. No."*

"She isn't ready!"

"Oh really? Then why is she on a date right now?" Alex's red eyes gleamed with satisfaction. He *knew* she was the one to set up that date. She had to be. Hele never would have done it on her own. She wouldn't seek out another when she'd Chosen him.

But do I know that for sure?

Could he have pushed her so far? She had never shown interest in anyone. He'd just assumed that her lack of romantic life meant she wasn't ready to pursue that part of herself yet, if ever. It was another reason for him to assume she wasn't ready, only reinforced by the sudden shocking interest she had in *him*. It seemed to come out of nowhere.

But... what if he was wrong?

Vael felt suddenly like the floor was giving way beneath his boots. Had he misjudged things? He only wanted the best for Hele. He wanted her to live her life to the fullest. He wanted her every breath to be joy, her every thought to be as bright as the lightning she created. He thought he knew what was necessary to make that possible.

But what if I've been wrong?

Did it even really matter? Even if he *was* right, that didn't change the fact that his Hele was currently out with another man. His mate might be getting her first kiss from someone else right at that moment. Maybe more.

She might be in danger.

It didn't matter that they'd been at peace with the elves for over a hundred years. He would never trust an elf he didn't know with the being who meant the most to him in the entire world.

Vael felt his breath shorten as instinct battled with self-discipline.

Instinct demanded he shift and scour the skies for his mate. It told him to sweep her up into his claws before he set fire to the puny little elf who dared set his sights on a mate already claimed.

Self-discipline knew that was a terrible plan. If there was an elf in the heart of the 'Riik, it was probably because he was part of a diplomatic entourage, making his roasting politically unfortunate. He also doubted that Hele would appreciate it.

But what could he do? Let his mate go? Let her be with another? Let her be endangered?

No. That's not a fucking option.

"Ah, that's right." Alex leaned back slowly. Her expression melted into something smug when she crossed her arms over her chest. "That look on your face — you just realized how badly you fucked up, didn't you? You don't even know the half of it, big man."

Vael raked his claws through his hair and pulled. His wings quivered. "There's *more?*"

"Oh yeah. Did you know she had a meeting with some witches today?" She polished the backs of her painted claws on a fold of her sash, then inspected her work. Speaking casually, like she wasn't kicking the shit out of him with every word, she continued, "Well, they were *so* impressed with her that one of them offered to help her get into some fancy university over in the Collective. Hele's thinking of taking her up on it. You know, since she has no reason to stay."

She... wants to leave?

His Hele wanted to leave the Draakonriik because of *him.*

Vael felt sick. He wanted her to fly, but not like this. This felt like running.

Hele never should have felt like she needed to flee — from anything, anyone, but most especially *him.*

His voice came out like crushed gravel when he asked again, "Where is she, Alex?"

"Why should I tell you? I'm loyal to her, not you."

"I love her." He couldn't think of what else could compel her to give him the information. What was more important than that? The *elf* didn't love her. The elf didn't even know her. Vael loved her so much that he felt like he'd been turned inside out by it.

Too bad Alex wasn't exactly the sentimental type.

She rolled her eyes. "Well, since you keep saying you *Chose* her, I should hope so—" A jaunty notification tone cut her off.

Holding up a finger and ignoring Vael's gnashing teeth, she sauntered over to her purse to dig out her cellphone. A huge, mischievous grin broke out across her face when she peered at the screen. "Oh, look! Speak of the elemental... Oh."

Dread fell heavily into his gut when Alex's expression morphed into one of deep worry. "What?" he barked, hurrying over to where she stood by the door. "What is it? What's wrong?"

When she didn't answer quickly enough, Vael hissed and simply snatched the phone from her hand. His eyes darted over the screen. The words splintered into nothing but broken glass as his grip tightened.

And then he saw red.

～

Hele knew the date was a bad idea.

While she thought that Alex had a point, and that it was good to follow through on her threat, she knew she'd made a mistake as soon as she left her apartment in her favorite dress.

The dress wasn't the problem. In fact, it was rather lovely — a treasured gift from her mother. Layers of gauzy purple fabric swirled around her calves when she walked, and the top was secured with a bow around her neck, leaving her back and arms free of constricting fabric. Paired with some sparkly flats and a very carefully secured hair clip by her ear, Hele felt lovely.

On the outside.

Inside, she didn't feel good about it at all. She'd never been on a date before, though it was one of those things she longed to experience, and she was nervous meeting someone she knew nothing about. There was a part of her that ached with curiosity, but mostly she was anxious. Most of the people she encountered were clanmates or worked for the 'Riik in some way. They were safe and within the realm of things she understood.

But a stranger? An *elf*?

Hele only knew of them from what she'd read and watched. Most of that was not exactly complimentary. According to an article she'd skimmed, they had only just recently begun mating outside of their ranks. She knew they were secretive, powerful, and vicious. Unlike herself and the dragons she knew, they only had the one form. Rather than making them weak, however, it seemed they made up for this disadvantage by being almost indestructible.

The pictures she'd seen, and the very few elves she'd glimpsed from afar, told her that they were a beautiful people — richly colored and varied like her dragons were — but terrifying. Something in their bearing said *back off or I'll bite*.

The man she'd been set up with was no different.

He was the EVP embassy's junior public liaison and knew Alex through a friend of a friend. Jacques was a pale green, with wavy hair he styled long at the top and short on the sides. He wore a pin-stripe suit and long coat. A collar was buttoned tight just under his chin. When he took her hand, it was with fingers swathed in leather and tipped with silver claws.

Wrong, something deep in her decided. *He is wrong.*

The wrong green. The wrong eyes. The wrong hands and scent and expression. Everything about him was wrong.

Not Vael. Not right.

Things only got worse when he leaned in close and took a

deep breath. Hele stood still, confused and a little put off by his intrusion into her space, until he slowly eased back. He looked... disappointed.

But the expression quickly smoothed over. An easy smile took its place, revealing four sharp fangs. Releasing her hand, he gave her a *stay here* gesture.

"I'll go see if they have a table available," he said. It was Friday night, and the steakhouse Alex had arranged for them to meet at was quite busy. There was a waiting area just beyond the doors, but it was packed with people. Hele was relieved to have an excuse to stay away from so many strangers who might gawk at her. She didn't go to restaurants without her family often, and now that she stood outside of one, she was reminded why.

Not only did she generally avoid food, but people *stared*.

"I'll wait here," she'd promised him, shifting slightly to one side to keep from blocking the door.

Jacques nodded once and then slipped inside. She breathed a sigh of relief, happy to be away from all the *wrong* for just a moment, and watched the busy downtown street as she waited for him to return.

She waited.

And waited.

When fifteen minutes crawled by, she peered through the doors and into the waiting area. There was no flash of pale green, or even the elegant shape of his narrow back. A few of the people had left, presumably escorted to tables, but there was no elf.

Maybe he went to the restroom?

Hele moved back into her place by the door. More people arrived, filing one by one into the steakhouse, and a few left, their eyes shiny and their laughter loud.

A half hour passed.

Forty-five minutes.

Confused and getting increasingly worried, Hele slipped into the restaurant to ask if the maitre d' had seen an elf come or go.

Did he ask about the restroom? Did he have an emergency of some kind?

Looking frazzled, the woman at the podium had distractedly answered, "No, the only elf I saw tonight came in and asked if he could use our back door." She shrugged. "He tipped well."

Hele felt a wave of pins and needles rush over her skin. "Oh."

She hurried outside then, dodging a small family with two pre-teens and an elder, to message Alex. Was this normal? Would he come back? Had she done something wrong?

Sure, she didn't want to go out with him in the first place, but even *she* knew that it wasn't good to be left at the door before the date even started. All she'd done was introduce herself.

Hele wracked her mind, combing through every second of their interaction as she waited for her sister to text her back with instructions. Insecurities rushed in alongside a heavy dose of indignation. What was so wrong with her that men kept rejecting her? It had to be something specific to her. She had trouble imagining *anyone* doing this to Alex.

It must have been something in her speech, or perhaps her looks that put the elf off so badly he needed to escape through a *back door.*

Hele hated that it wounded her.

She didn't even know the man. She certainly didn't want him in any sexual or romantic sense, and yet it *hurt* to know she was so strange that he couldn't bear to even pretend to like her for an evening.

Eyes stinging, she wrapped her arms around herself and sank onto the curb by the entrance. Her sparkly shoes, a favorite pair she'd picked out herself, looked garish in the gutter. Hele sniffed hard and wished that she had never agreed to such a ridiculous idea.

She felt terribly alone as people drifted around her, on their way to spend evenings with the people they loved. It was ugly — this miasma of loneliness, rejection, and directionless failure. The feeling came from a deep place, before she knew words or time. It came from the *before,* when she was boundless, and it was terrible.

I want to go home, she thought. But where was home? Not her family's nest. Not her empty apartment. Home was a man that made the world seem quieter, softer.

She squeezed her eyes shut. The spinning feeling, like everything was too much, too fast, grated on her nerves like sharpened claws. It was all she could do to breathe and *wait.*

An ear-splitting roar carried over the lake like an explosion. All around her, heads lifted. Parents and those who protected their loved ones stilled, their eyes on the sky, before they began to hurry their people off of the street — into restaurants, vehicles, wherever there was shelter.

No one wanted to be out when an enraged dragon took to wing.

Hele barely noticed that the street emptied. She simply wrapped her arms around her knees and buried her head there, waiting for her cellphone to ping.

CHAPTER ELEVEN

VAEL FOUND HIS MATE SITTING ON THE CURB IN FRONT of a steakhouse. *Alone.*

Rage was a pulse in his mind, throbbing harder, faster, with every second that flashed by. His dark eyes fixed on the speck of white and purple a hundred feet below him. Banking hard on his massive, scarred wings, he glided in a circle, down, down, toward the nearly empty street.

Fire licked up his throat, blisteringly cold. It wanted *out.*

It wanted to burn the entire street to ash. Dragonfire could burn for days, for *years* if properly fed. It had a peculiar chemical property specific to dragons that made it feel ice cold even as it burned you into nothing but bubbling fat and splintered bone. Let loose on the street, there would be nothing left to salvage. It was a lucky thing that he had no desire to burn his mate.

The dragon, not the man, was in control as he arrowed down toward his Hele.

Find my mate. Hide her in our nest.

His eyes were locked on her form, huddled as it was, as he glided down, wings held taut as he slowed. Her body language was one of a wounded creature. Balled up, like she expected pain and could only *endure.* It was the same way she used to curl up when they brought her to the 'Riik. She used to make herself small, and when he held her, she shook. She'd made so much progress since then. Seeing her back in that place was... *horrible.*

Vael, already on the edge, spiraled out of control.

A larger than average dragon, he landed in the middle of the street with enough force to rattle windows and set off car alarms. Still, Hele did not look up. Her slim arms contracted around her knees. Her hair, normally so full of movement and electricity, lay limp around her in a pool of dull white.

Moving on four scaled limbs rather than two, Vael hurtled down the road. He felt eyes on him from the shops and restaurant windows. Opening his jaws and mantling his wings in a display of dangerous dragon territoriality, he let loose a subvocal growl that warned every living creature within a mile radius *not to fuck with him.*

Drawing close, he huffed out a smoky breath and tried to find calm. Hele looked so small when he was in his quadrupedal form. If she were human, she would have been considered quite tall, but compared to him — shifted or not — she was delicate.

Like *this,* she looked as fragile as spun glass.

Vael lowered his head as he approached. His growl died away, replaced by a soft crooning note. He lifted his wings high and arched them around her, creating a semi-enclosed tent over her huddled form. The light from the streetlamps filtered in through the thin membrane of his wings to cast dark red and gold shapes on the crown of her head.

Desperate to be close, to inspect her for injuries he couldn't immediately see, Vael brought his snout down to ruffle her hair. His breath, icy cold, *whuffed* out. She smelled like rain and fresh, tart strawberries. There was no blood, but elves were capable of so much more than cuts. What if her date hadn't just abandoned her? What if he touched her without consent? What if he bruised her?

Vael's pupils contracted into quivering lines so thin, they were barely discernible against the dark green of his irises. Rage and fear for his mate made his huge body shake.

Only Hele's sudden movement stopped him from lifting his snout to the sky to let out a roar that would have shattered eardrums — a warning to the bastard that a dragon was coming for him.

Without lifting her head, Hele snaked her arms around his neck. Her palms settled in the sensitive spots behind his horns. Breathing heavily, she rested her temple against the curve of his jaw and whispered, "I just wanted to go on a date. I don't understand what I did wrong. He didn't *explain*."

Motherfucker!

Vael vividly remembered her early days when she demanded an explanation for everything, when her most used words were *why* and *how*. His Hele hated feeling like she didn't know what to do or why people acted the way they did. Asking questions was her way of taking control of a situation. When people didn't bother to explain things to her or brushed her aside, he'd seen her shrink into herself, self-conscious. To know that she'd been *stood up* and then insulted in the way that stung her the most...

I'm going to fucking kill him.

His wings flexed as the hunting instinct bore down on him. Instinct screamed. It narrowed his focus to a pinprick, a dark tunnel with only one focus—

Hele sniffled.

And just like that, Vael's violent rage melted into a new shape: *protectiveness.*

He couldn't communicate with her in this form — not verbally, at least — but he could take care of her. He had to, seeing as he didn't quite have the control necessary to shift back yet. He wouldn't until he had her sequestered, *safe.*

Forcefully shaking off the bloody rage that consumed him, Vael made another soft noise in the back of his throat and very gently nuzzled the side of her head. He felt the silk of her hair sliding against his tough dragon hide and thought, *This is my fault.*

Regret burned like bile up the back of his throat. If he hadn't been so bullheaded, he could have saved her this pain. She would never have run off to experience something with another man. He could have given her the best first date imaginable. He could have done *so much* for her, but he was so wrapped up in what he thought she needed that he pushed her into seeking out someone else.

And now she was hurt. *Because of me.*

It was unbearable.

Instinct demanded he take her back to their nest and see to her care. He had to make things right between them. He had to make sure she knew that there would never be a need to find another. There would be no more dates with elves. No more of this awful pain. No more sitting on a curb alone, waiting for some asshole, while the world stared.

Skinning the elf alive and then cooking him like second rate chuck roast would have to wait.

Extending one clawed foreleg, Vael oh-so-carefully nudged her into a more upright sitting position. Hele leaned back to give him a view of her tear-streaked face and wobbling chin.

My fucking heart, he thought, gasping for breath like it could ease the guilt, the anger that choked him. His tail — huge, muscled, and lined with deadly spikes — thrashed over the gritty asphalt. Somewhere behind him a trash can toppled over and rolled away.

"What?" she asked, brows bunching together.

Vael couldn't help but lower his head to trace her cheek with the tip of his nose. His tongue snaked out, quick as Hele's lightning, to lick away her tears. She sputtered and her arms fell away from his neck. He took the opportunity to nod toward the night sky.

Fly, he tried to tell her. *Fly with me.*

He held his breath as he waited for her response. Hele

scrubbed at her face with her palms. A little bit of spark returned to her hair when she muttered, "No. I won't go with you. I like this dress. I don't want to lose it."

He let out an exasperated huff and nodded again, more insistent this time.

"Are you going to try and escort me back to my family's nest?" Her expression darkened. Crossing her arms, she informed him, "I don't need you to rescue me *or* take me back to my parents. I'm fine. Alex will come get me soon."

Vael disagreed with that assessment very much, but he knew that stubborn thrust of her chin well. Of course, she didn't know that Alex would not be coming to get her. Not just because he'd destroyed her phone, either.

She'd rightfully given him shit for what happened with Hele, but when it came to *this,* she was still a dragon — and every dragon knew not to step between mates. If she came between them now, Vael wasn't entirely sure that he would be able to keep his instinct to protect his mate in check. Luckily, she knew better.

Since he knew Alex wouldn't be coming, he nudged his mate again.

"No." Her chin jutted in that way he loved. Unfortunately, it also signaled that she'd dug her heels in. Hele had made up her mind and would not be following him anywhere.

Eyeing her lithe frame, he thought, *Well, if she won't follow me...*

Ignoring Hele's surprised grunt, Vael gently wrapped his claws around her middle and lifted her off of the ground. The surprised look on her face was absolutely priceless.

"What are you *doing?*" If she had looked panicked, he would have put her down immediately, but Hele looked more delighted than afraid as he began to quickly, if not gracefully, make his way to the tall perch at the end of the street. Designed for heavy-bodied dragons in either form, public perches were legally required to be installed every four blocks in towns and cities of the Draakonriik.

Was it comfortable climbing up to the top with his mate carefully cradled in his palm? No, but if he could do it with broken limbs and bolt gun wounds, he could manage *this*.

It helped that he knew if she somehow fell, Hele would be fine. She could dematerialize in half a second. That didn't mean he would risk it, though.

Vael clutched her close to his chest as he climbed the five story tower. His heartbeat thundered when he felt her tiny hands smooth over his hide, leaving trails of sparks in their wake. She could have slipped his grasp if she truly wanted to, but he guessed his Hele was too curious about what he intended to do to try it.

He would reward that curiosity and her trust later. *Now* he had to get her home.

Pulling his hulking body over the edge of the platform, Vael stopped for just a moment to run his nose over the top of her head and down her back, soothing himself, before he ambled over to the edge. He felt her shift against him, perhaps to peer out, before her fingers flexed on the corded muscles of his long neck.

A great swell of tenderness filled his chest. Wishing he could speak with her mind to mind, he thought, *I have you, my fallen star. You are safe.*

Holding her tight to his breast, Vael threw them off of the perch.

Chapter Twelve

THEIR ROOST WAS ONLY A FIFTEEN MINUTE FLIGHT from downtown De Tour, but it felt like the longest flight of his life. Longer, even, than his first painful flight after a year of recovery and physical therapy.

His mate was in his grasp, trusting him to hold her as he sailed through the crisp night air. His mate curled her arms around his neck and held on when he banked, catching a current. His mate tucked her head against his throat and curled up in his claws, mirroring the moment they met.

I have her, he repeated to himself over and over. *I will fix this. She will be happy again. After, I will hunt the elf. All will be well.*

He felt her sit up a little when their roost came into view. Located on a tiny island in the middle of Lake Michigan, it would have been easy to miss if he hadn't installed the required warning lights along the roof and sturdy perch.

Built in the style of traditional dragonish architecture, it was a tall stone structure that called to mind an eclectic mix of old world cathedral and new age skyscraper. Several stories tall but narrow, it stuck out like a flint blade from the craggy rocks and lush green foliage of the island. In the heart of winter, when freezing water whipped off of the lake and gale force winds buffeted the reinforced walls, it became coated in ice — transforming it into a glittering spire.

Vael banked again, bringing them down slowly toward the perch. He felt Hele lean forward and then— "Oh! My shoe!"

He glanced down just in time to see one of her sparkly flats slip off her foot. It spiraled in the air, caught a draft, and then careened toward the frothy water. Without thinking, Vael lunged.

Wings jackknifing out to stop their descent, his back legs just skimmed the water as he snatched the shoe out of the air.

Hele squealed. "Do not drop me! I don't understand swimming!"

Never, he thought. His claws tightened around her even as he did a quick, expert roll over the waves. Water misted them both, icy cold and sweet.

It stirred something dark and pleasurable in him when he heard Hele gasp. A peal of laughter quickly followed it. Savoring her joy as the balm it was, Vael pumped his wings, caught another updraft, and sailed around their roost once more.

He landed with a *thump* on the perch. Carefully, he lowered his leg and unwrapped his claws from around his mate. She staggered for a moment, her normal quick grace absent, as she found her footing on the cold platform. One wee foot was bare. Her toes peeked out from under the soft layers of her skirt as she took half a step back.

Giving her a toothy, dragon grin, he dropped her fallen shoe at her feet.

Hele looked down at it and blinked, her expression as unsure as he'd ever seen it. "You didn't have to do that," she said, voice trembling faintly. "It was just a shoe."

Magic crackled around him — hot, wild. It broke his bones, peeled his skin, bubbled up and out to tear him apart and remake him an instant. One moment he was the size of a small plane, the next he was a man standing before her.

His voice was raspy when he answered, "Of course I had to. It's one of your favorites."

She started. "You remember?"

"My Hele..." He swallowed hard. Cold, wet wind buffeted his bare back, but he didn't feel it. "I remember *everything*."

"Oh." There was so much in that soft sound, but he couldn't decipher what any of it was. Hele's eyes were pure black, with neither pupil nor whites, so it was often hard to pick up on her expressions if one didn't know where to look. He had spent two years learning her cues, but at that moment, he was utterly at a loss.

Wrapping her arms around herself, she turned slowly to peer at the arched glass door that led into the anteroom. "Where are we? I thought you were going to drag me back to my *ema*." She looked up, and in a softer voice added, "This place is beautiful."

Vael moved behind her. It took several steadying breaths to drive off the impulse to wrap his arms around her waist and draw her back against his nude form. *Just to hold her. To know she's here. She's safe.*

Despite his restraint, there was little to be done about his errant tail. If ever dragons had a *tell*, it was their *tail*. The damn things always had a mind of their own. His snaked over his thigh to curl around her delicately wrought knee.

Mine, it said. *And I'm not letting you go.*

When she didn't brush him off, Vael felt some of the painful tension in his shoulders ease. "This is my dwelling." He paused, weighing his words, before he forced out, "This is *our* dwelling."

"Now or later?"

If he could have punched the Vael from that afternoon in the side of the head, he would have. Instead, he firmly answered, *"Always."*

Hele gave him another fathomless look. When she continued to say nothing, Vael ran his fingers through his spiky hair and let out a short sigh. He stooped to pick up her fallen shoe.

"Come on," he murmured, gesturing for her to walk toward the sliding door. "Let's get you inside, *täht*."

She didn't protest as he led her through the door and into the anteroom. The back of his neck heated as that dark, twisty feeling of pleasure bloomed again. *My mate in my nest.*

It was where she belonged, and everything in him knew it. Finally, he felt like he could rest.

Now I just have to find a way to convince her to stay.

Looking at her now, when she still clutched at her sides and looked at him like she had no idea what to make of him, he wasn't at all sure it would be an easy task. *Fool,* he thought for the thousandth time that evening. *You could have had her here last night, if you'd just listened to what she was trying to tell you.*

But that was the past, and Vael did his best to not dwell on what he could not change. It hadn't brought his parents back to life, nor his grandparents. It hadn't fixed his destroyed home. It hadn't fixed his wings, or returned his voice.

Only moving forward brought peace. Only determination and loyalty won him happiness.

Why would it not be the same with his Hele? But first...

Vael circled around her, utterly unselfconscious of his nudity, to stare into her eyes. Brows lowering, he asked, "What happened tonight?"

She shrugged, quick and jerky. "Nothing."

"Hele."

"Vael."

He lifted his hands, desperate to grasp her arms and draw her close, but forced himself to lower them again. Behind him, his wings flexed hard. "Did that elf hurt you? Tell me, *täht.*"

"Hurt me?" She made a face. "No. He only shook my hand before he— wait. How did you know I was on a date with an elf?"

He felt his temper bubble with the reminder that she was on a *date* with *another man* — who fucking ditched her! — but kept a ruthless grip on the desire to rage. It was what he'd pushed her to. What right did he have to be jealous?

Every right, instinct roared. *She is my mate!*

It was a common misconception that dragons became possessive of their Chosen mates out of some greedy desire to *hoard.*

While it was true that his kind loved shiny and silky things, the acquisitive impulse did not translate to matehood.

Dragons were aggressively territorial of their mates for the same reasons other beings were, but also because when they *Chose,* the pathways in their minds that navigated the magnetic field of the Earth rewired to make their mate *home.* When he called Hele his north star, his *täht,* it was not just because of how she was brought into the world. It was quite literally what she was.

For a dragon, all flights led back to their Chosen. All comfort, security, and warmth could be found in them. They *were* the roost, the nest.

Was it not understandable, he wondered, that they would have such a visceral reaction to a perceived threat or interloper?

But he was not just instinct and tangled neural pathways forged over millennia. He was a man, and though he was hard headed, he knew when it was imperative that he keep his cool.

Forcing the words out from between gritted fangs, he answered, "Your sister told me."

"Alex?" Hele's expression fell, then tightened again with heart-breaking betrayal. "Why would she tell you that?"

"I believe she was trying to taunt me." And it worked. Not only because he was possessive, but because of a past she almost certainly didn't know.

If she knew it was elves who shelled his family's dwelling, he was certain she would not have thrown it in his face. Alex would have been horrified to know it was glamoured elves who sifted through the rubble of his small town to execute those who survived. It was elves who haunted his nightmares.

The thought of his Hele, untried, trusting, with an elf who could tear her limb from limb... It was too much for him to handle. It would have been bad if it was *anyone* on a date with her, but an elf? Unreasonable panic made his hands shake.

He wasn't trapped in the rubble. He was fine. But that feeling of imminent death, the *loss...* That lingered like a stain in his soul, tainting everything it touched. The desperation he felt, the fear of losing his clan again, was too much to ignore.

One way or another, he could have lost his mate. All because he thought he knew what she needed — even when she told him what she *wanted*.

Hele looked up at him with a small frown. "I did not want her to do that. I just wanted—" She stopped herself. Her lips, soft and faintly purple, pressed into a hard line.

His heart ached for her. Lowering his voice, he asked, "Tell me, *täht*. What did you want?"

When she spoke, her voice was hollow, tired. "I just wanted to *see*. I wanted to know what it was like to go on a date. But I didn't go on a date. He thought I was— I must be awful, because he did not even want to pretend. He paid someone to let him out the backdoor."

Her chin wobbled again, but his stubborn, proud Hele did not let herself cry. Squaring her shoulders, she said, "I didn't even like him. He was *wrong*. But I think I am done with dates. I'll just have to find a mate another way."

Blood rushed in his ears. "You will not."

"I *will*."

"You won't because you *have* a mate." He stepped closer, until their bodies nearly touched. The anger was back, but not directed at her. It burned as cold and vicious as dragon fire in his veins when he ground out, "Your *mate* will hunt this elf down and bring you his fucking head."

Hele didn't have the same eyes as him, so it was hard to tell for certain, but he *knew* she rolled them then. The sad creature on the curb was gone. Vivid life had returned alongside her temper. Her hair swayed against her back, the strands popping and sizzling with the power he loved so much. "I do not want his head!"

He breathed deep and held the air in his lungs. *Calm. Hele is what matters. You must be calm.*

Temper momentarily banked, he dared to skim the tip of his

nose over hers, then down across her cheek. Breathing against her dainty ear, he asked, "Then what *do* you want?"

For once, she had no quick comeback for him. Vael felt her sway slightly, closer to him, giving him the chance to hear her breath hitch.

His lashes brushed the sweet curve of her cheek when he whispered, "You Chose me, Hele. I think you know what — *who* you want. This fight is done. You've won it. I'm yours."

"I didn't. You said *no*. You said *not yet*." The tremble in her voice nearly killed him. "I didn't win anything. My mate doesn't want me. That's not *winning*."

He allowed himself the small comfort of touching his forehead to her temple, right where the wispy hairs turned into long, bone white strands. "I'm sorry. To know I've made you feel this way, when all I've ever wanted is your happiness— Hele, I never meant to hurt you. You have to know by now how much I *do* want you. Enough to wait as long as you needed me to. I thought I was doing what was right."

"*For* me." She practically spat the words. They hit him in two pitiless blows, making him wince.

"Yes," he answered. "And that was wrong. I should have listened."

His proud mate did not give an inch. "You should have."

"Do you forgive me, my mate?"

"I haven't decided."

Gods, I love you, you stubborn woman. Never change.

Was it wrong to smile when he was apologizing? Vael bit the insides of his cheeks. He loved her pride so much. He didn't even mind that she was upset with him still. She had a right to be. He was happy to beg for forgiveness, so long as she stayed with him.

If this was crawling, as Artem suggested he should, then he didn't think he minded it too much. He loved her spirit. His wily mate made him proud every time she fought for herself, when she defiantly showed her spark to the world.

"Let me make it up to you, *täht.*"

"I do not think I should."

"Why not?"

"Because..." She paused, clearly searching for reasons to deny him. "Because I have decided to mate with one of mine. I do not want a dragon."

Banking his instinctive, explosive reaction to her challenge, toothless as he felt it was, Vael skimmed her bare arm with his palm. He didn't touch her, but held his hand close enough to feel their shared heat when he coaxed, "Then there is no harm, is there? If you won't Choose me again, why not let me apologize in my way? You've made up your mind, after all. Wouldn't you let a friend make it up to you?"

He *loved* her little growl. He was fairly sure it wasn't something that came naturally to elementals. She must have picked it up from her clanmates. He was glad she did. That tiny, kitten's growl made lust skitter down his spine as readily as her sparks did.

Finally, after a long, stubborn silence, she begrudgingly asked, "What will you do?"

Vael let his grin spread. It was one part relieved and one part *hungry*. "Nothing painful," he promised. "I just want a date."

Chapter Thirteen

Hele wondered if she'd made a mistake.

Alex would not have said yes to this.

Her sister would have brushed Vael off and flown out the door, entirely unbothered by his pleas for forgiveness. Hele wondered if that was the right way to handle this situation or simply her sister's preferred method.

Truthfully, she wasn't sure about *anything* anymore.

What she *did* know was that she *did not* want to go. For all her big talk, the idea of leaving Vael to return to her lonely little dwelling made her insides curdle. It would have been even worse to return to her parents. She did not want to have to explain to her parents why she was upset.

She felt too tender inside. It was like she had been pricked all over by tiny needles and now she was raw. All she wanted to do was curl up in a dark room, bury her face in Vael's neck, and be *still*.

That was not what he had in mind for their *date*, though.

After kicking off her remaining shoe by the door, Hele followed him warily through his dwelling. She begrudgingly admitted to herself that it was much nicer than her little apartment, cute though it was.

For one thing, it was *huge*. For another, the muted tones of the furniture and the soft green walls felt like him in a way she couldn't quite put her finger on. Everything felt soft. Comfortable. Calm. Except...

"How long have you lived here?"

Vael guided her down a hall that opened up into a spiral staircase. She did her best to keep her eyes from wandering down his naked back, but it wasn't easy. The eye was naturally drawn to the swish-flick of a tail, particularly when it rested above a tightly muscled backside. *You should not look at him that way,* she stubbornly reminded herself. *He isn't your mate.*

It was easier said than done. She'd been ogling Vael since she first learned what ogling *was*. Trying to stop herself now was simply unnatural.

"I bought the original dwelling a year ago and have been renovating and adding onto it ever since." He glanced over one broad shoulder to give her a hopeful, searching look. "What do you think of it?"

Even when she was angry at him, Hele couldn't bear to crush the hope she saw shining in his eyes. "It is a very nice dwelling." She skimmed her palm over the smooth metal railing. "But it doesn't feel very..."

He paused mid-step and waited for her to draw even with him. His tail looped loosely around her leg, briefly distracting her. A rush of tingles washed through her. Vael had gone from never touching her to almost constant skin contact. She knew that she should not relish it, but she did all the same.

Touch was *lovely* — but only when Vael did it.

As was his new habit, he leaned in close and pressed, "What? Is there something wrong with it?"

If there was one thing she learned very early on, it was never to insult a dragon's dwelling. Staring down at the dark purple tail gently caressing her ankle, she carefully answered, "No. Nothing is wrong with it."

His tail gave her a quick squeeze. Hele's eyes moved up, over strong calves, thick thighs, a fascinating cock, a muscled waist, and finally to his frowning face. "It's okay, Hele. You can tell me."

She scuffed her bare foot against the edge of the step. "I don't know if this is the right way to say it, but it does not *feel* like you have lived here for a year."

There was a strange sort of stiffness to the air in the house. It didn't feel as lived in as her parents' dwelling, or even Alex's. While Hele did not necessarily know what *made* a house feel lived in, she felt its absence all the same.

Instead of being offended, Vael simply smiled ruefully and hovered his big, warm palm over the small of her back, urging her onward without really touching her — save for his tail. "That's because I don't actually spend much time here. Haven't had a reason to. I usually sleep in the barracks."

Hele blinked. "Why? If you didn't want to sleep in your dwelling, why did you buy one?"

They came upon a landing, but Vael didn't stop there. His fingertips brushed her hip, telling her wordlessly to keep going. Another landing. More stairs. Another. The air began to cool as they descended.

His voice was a deep rumble when he finally answered, "I needed to have a roost, but sleeping here is difficult for me."

"Why?"

The stairs ended. The polished wood and metal steps melted into small, iridescent tiles shaped like coins. Hele stared down the short hallway. The air on the bottom floor was different. Strangely warmer than in the stairway. It sat heavily on her tongue, and had a funny, salty tang.

Water. It tasted like water, but not the lake's particular, earthy flavor she was used to.

Before she could try and guess what in the world lay at the end of the dark hall, Vael came up behind her. His hands cupped her arms — holding without actually touching — and his heat radiated along her spine. Her breath snagged in her throat. His spicy scent enveloped her, overtaking that salty water to fill up her senses with *him*.

His voice was soft and whispery. "I bought this dwelling for you, Hele. I can't sleep in it without you."

Oh. Her heart began to pound. A little bit more of the starch left her spine, but not enough to bend her will completely. Just to be contrary, she breathily replied, "I don't sleep, you know."

"I know." Were those his lips pressed against the shell of her ear? Goosebumps broke out all over her body. The scent of him, the way his chest brushed her back, it all made heat coil low in her belly. The feeling made her restless. Unsettled. It was like pressure, but not quite.

It was utterly unique — just like everything she felt for him.

Slowly, he began to walk them down the shadowed hallway. With each step, he breathed another word into her ear. "You think I don't remember everything about you, my Hele? Every single one of my thoughts has been yours since the moment I caught you." A shiver raced down her spine when he used the very tip of one claw to brush a lock of hair away from her neck. His breath, hot and humid as the water-heavy air, puffed against her skin when he continued, "I've spent months making sure this dwelling suits your needs, my mate. I've gotten you the nicest blankets. The softest pillows. I've dreamed of what you'll look like laid out on them, ready for me."

Hele had to brace one hand on the wall to steady herself. How wonderful and frightening it was to feel like her body had a mind of its own! Her knees felt strangely weak. Her blood rushed in her ears. Her sex pulsed with every beat of her heart, building a deep, pleasurable ache.

Words tumbled from her lips, though she did not know where they came from, seeing as her head was full of lust's fog. "You built this place for *my* needs?"

She was *certain* she felt the smallest, lightest kiss to the whorl of her ear then. "Yes."

She didn't understand why her voice shook when she asked, "H-how?"

Hele thought she *felt* the smile curving his lips. "For starters, I built you a library."

She stumbled on the smooth tiles just before the door. "You *what?*"

Claws curled around the bulk of her hair just at the base of her head, gathering it in a firm but gentle grip. Vael's other hand pushed open the plain metal door as he ran the tip of his nose over her cheek. There was a strange, husky note in his voice when he answered, "A library. For you. Here."

Hele barely registered the dim room he'd led her into. She stared sightlessly at the small lap pool in the center, glowing pale aquamarine in the gossamer dark. Steam curled from the surface like wisps of smoke. She couldn't fathom why he'd brought her there, but she also didn't care.

"A library? With *paper* books?"

Vael used his grip on her hair to slowly turn her head to one side. When she caught his eye, she found his gaze half-lidded and his smile predatory. Was that supposed to thrill her, or was this yet another way she was a little bit wrong?

Vael had never been anything other than gentle with her and she *loved* that, but when he looked at her like he wanted to *eat* her... Well, Hele learned something new about herself every day.

"Paper books," he purred. "Whenever I go on a trip with Taevas, I try to visit a shop for you. I usually come home with a whole suitcase full of books."

Was she panting? It felt like she was panting. Hele struggled to get her excitement under control.

She didn't manage to succeed even a little bit.

But... *paper* books? Hele only had a handful of those. Most books were digital, which was extremely convenient and made searching for specific subjects or terms easy for her. On the other hand, she had learned that books had only recently been digitized. While many, many thousands were accessible to her, there were untold *millions* in the world which would likely never exist on her tablet's screen for one reason or another. The idea of lost knowledge locked in ephemera drove her *wild.*

If there was one thing Hele couldn't stand, it was the idea that there was a part of life she was missing out on. Untapped knowledge had the same appeal to her as love. To her, they were one and the same.

What had he gotten for her? Her mind raced with the possibilities. At least once a week he'd sent books to her tablet — classics, fascinating narrative history, science, humor, and even some strange science fiction that made her giggle. She was *dying* to see what treasures he'd collected for her in paper and ink.

She bounced on the balls of her feet, her hair snapping and twisting in the humid air with her unconcealed glee. "Can I see?"

Vael's eyes crinkled with his smile. "After."

"After *what?*"

Giving her hair a playful little tug, he said, "Our date!"

She made a face. "This isn't a date. Those are outside."

"Says who?"

"Says... my books. And Alex!"

"A date can be anything, as long as it's something you do with a person you care about." His expression darkened, and she caught the motion of a lashing tail out of the corner of her eye. "I will take you on another date after this. The best date you can imagine. *Outside.* "

It was on the tip of her tongue to say this was already better than anything she could imagine, but she kept the words in out of pure stubbornness. It wouldn't do to let him think he'd been forgiven just because he'd given her everything she yearned for.

Even if it *was* true.

"Well, if we aren't going to see the library, then what *are* we doing?" she asked, feeling suddenly quite mulish. What in the world could be better than a library? *Nothing.*

He released her hair and stepped around her. His skin, shifted to a deep red-violet with the sunset, looked otherworldly in the pale blue-green glow of the pool. She tilted her head, admiring him unabashedly. She loved that Vael had two tiny gold hoops in the lobes of his ears. They flashed against the darkness of his skin. *Like my sparks.*

He swept his arm out toward the pool and he told her, "I'm giving you a swim lesson."

CHAPTER FOURTEEN

"Get in the water, *taht.*"

"No."

The warm saltwater flowed around his wings as he drifted toward the edge of the pool. It was incredibly tempting to reach out and cover her bare feet with his hands, slick and warm from the water. Then he could just slip his claws up, over the slopes of her delicate ankles, and up, up, up...

Not now.

Vael smothered his low burning arousal with ruthless efficiency, just like every other time he enjoyed Hele's company in the two years he'd known her. It was never easy, but now that he knew she wanted him, and he'd finally given himself the freedom to woo her, it took every ounce of self control he possessed to keep the touch-hunger at bay.

Gods, I want to devour her.

Even when she stared down at him with that scowl, her arms crossed and her brow crinkled, he wanted to slide his head between her thighs and greet paradise.

"The water is warm," he cajoled, voice roughened with lust he couldn't quite contain. "There's nothing to be afraid of."

"I. Am. Electric." Hele bit the words off of the tip of her tongue. "I do not *swim.*"

"And I'm built for flight. I'm not supposed to swim either." To prove his point, he tipped backward, spread his wings, and began to float. He had to bite the insides of his cheeks again to withhold a smile when he watched Hele's attention drift down his body and back up again. Where her gaze lingered, his skin tingled, desperate for her touch.

His chest swelled with pride even as a new, more potent shot of lust forced him to lower his legs back down to the bottom of the pool. It wouldn't hide anything, really, but it wouldn't shove his half-hard cock in her face either.

Vael inwardly blanched. *Do not picture that!*

Blessedly, Hele distracted him from that devastating mental image by crouching down near the edge. Her dress pooled around her as she carefully rested her palms on her knees. Eyeing the water warily, she asked, "Why *do* you have a pool? I don't know any dragons who swim."

As much as he loved looking at her, Vael found his eyes moving away. He stared at the ceiling, covered in tiny reflective tiles that seemed to move with the rippling image of the water below, and watched the dark shapes of his wings flex in the water.

His throat felt tight with remembered pain when he quietly answered, "It's good for my wings. Water therapy is the only reason I can still fly today."

There was a brief pause, then, "Why? What happened to your wings?"

Why? He loved that word. It was the first real one she said to him. That didn't mean he was excited to answer her, though.

A surge of wild affection twined with deep reluctance. He hated telling the story of his injuries. It meant he had to share what happened to his clan, and that subject would always be too painful to bear. Mostly, he preferred to keep his silence. It was in the quiet moments that he felt them most.

But Hele needed to know who and what he was. She had

Chosen him, and that meant she belonged to his clan, too. It was her right to understand what had happened to the rest of them.

Still, he wasn't above using the story he didn't wish to tell as leverage. Knowing her voracious mind would jump at any chance to learn something new, he pushed himself back toward her side of the pool and held out his hands. "Come in and I'll tell you."

He watched her lips tighten. The look in her eyes dimmed from cautiously curious to simply sad. Quietly, she said, "I can't. Not with you."

"Why not?"

"Because water moves electricity," she answered, making a wavy motion with her hand. "I tried a bath once, but it went... badly. My *isa* told me that it is dangerous for others to be in water with me. It could stop a heart."

Stop a heart? Vael shook his head. "Constantin isn't wrong. You should probably never get in a body of water with anyone — *except* dragons."

Hele tilted her head to one side, clearly skeptical. "You have a heart, don't you?"

Trying to lighten her mood, Vael pressed his palm against his chest and sighed dramatically. "Ah, my Hele, I don't. I gave that to you a long time ago."

The telltale sign that his mate was fighting a smile? Her full lower lip thrust out in a little pout that drove him absolutely insane. He wanted to take that lip and nibble on it with his fangs, then slowly slip his tongue into the silky well of her mouth and—

"Tell me the story."

He nonchalantly flicked at the warm, salty water with the tips of his claws. "I'm waiting for you to get in."

Watching her stomp one bare foot while she was crouched over the edge of the pool was the single most adorable thing he'd ever witnessed. "I *can't.*"

"You can," he insisted. "Hele, do you really think my skin can't stand some electricity? Dragons fly through lightning and m-storms regularly. *You* have shocked me dozens of times."

She huffed. "Those weren't shocks."

"Yeah? Then what were they? Kisses?"

He said it as a joke, but when Hele didn't respond, and instead looked away, Vael's mind stalled. *All those times she— no.*

Bracing his palms on either side of her, Vael surged upward until his upper body was completely out of the pool. Water droplets rained down on the glittery concrete and her bare toes. Eye to eye, he asked, *"Täht...* have you kissed me?"

"No," she muttered, sparks snapping wildly around her face and hair. "I *struck* you. It is the only— I do not know how to kiss like you mean. Striking is what I know."

He felt like he couldn't breathe. Vael wracked his mind, trying to remember all the times they'd flown together. Of course he noticed that she struck him — hard to miss a lightning bolt or ten — but he never considered it might be her way of expressing romantic affection. Playfulness, yes. But the elemental equivalent of a *kiss?*

The cogs in Vael's mind stalled again when he estimated the number of times she had struck him mid-flight.

Dozens. Dozens and dozens.

After a moment of intense thought, he slowly asked, "Don't you strike others?"

Hele's eyes narrowed. That dainty finger came out again, this time to poke him in the shoulder. Her sparks bit at his skin, sizzling in the tiny water droplets there. "I do *not* strike others. Only you. Gently."

His grin spread in tandem with his wings, which stretched out behind him in a quivering display of pride and affection. His voice was breathless when he confirmed, "You've *kissed* me. A *lot."*

Glory save me, my mate has been telling me how she feels for a year. *Longer, even.*

A look of irritation quickly covered up a flash of hurt in her eyes. "Well, you didn't notice, so it doesn't matter—"

He didn't give her time to finish the thought.

One of Vael's hands snapped up to curl around the back of

her neck. His tail sliced through the water behind him, and when he sucked in a deep breath of her through his nose, his whole body shook.

My mate. My beautiful, temperamental, incredible mate.

He crushed their lips together.

It was her first kiss. He was aware of that even as instinct demanded he *take*. Vael forced himself to hold still, to be gentle.

At first Hele was stiff, her lips sealed shut against his, but after a gentle, sucking kiss to that full bottom lip he loved so much, she began to relax. Her mouth opened just enough for him to feel her warmth, her breath. It was a little bit cooler than his own — like he was breathing in the cold, wet air of a brewing storm.

Perfect.

When he slowly dipped his tongue past her teeth, just for a taste, he was shocked to discover that she tasted like *rainwater*.

A feeling he couldn't describe took hold of his throat and crushed it. There was no way for her to know how wild that taste made him, the brutal memories it conjured.

One of the only reasons he survived in the rubble for as long as he did was because it rained. The water had flowed over the shattered stone of his clan's dwelling, running in tiny rivers down through the cracks that allowed him the smallest amount of smoky air. Trapped there, body broken, it was all he could do to tilt back his head and let the drops fall on his smoke-scorched tongue.

His Hele tasted like *life*.

Vael knew that he should be softer. It was her first real kiss. He should go slow, let her take the lead until she was comfortable.

But he couldn't. Not now. He couldn't taste rainwater, *her*, and not be driven out of his mind with the need to drink and drink and drink.

His grip tightened, pulling her closer as he slid his tongue against hers, exploring every new sensation and sweet sound she made. Her hands fluttered first around his shoulders before they settled on his jaw. She leaned in, deepening the kiss with a needy noise.

Like they had done this a thousand times, they fell into sync.

When he moved, so did she. When she breathed, he breathed. When he tugged her closer, closer, she leaned so far over the edge, her hair trailed into the pool.

And then they were both falling.

Vael's wings stretched out to nearly skim the sides of the pool as they hit the water. Hele's gauzy purple dress billowed around them, twining with the impossibly long stream of her hair.

He probably wouldn't have even noticed they were in the water at all if a massive electrical current hadn't made his body momentarily lock.

His back arched as the shock rolled through him, part pain and part pleasure. His cock jerked, sensitive skin and nerves over-stimulated to the point where he thought he might come from just *that*. He choked, fighting the pressure, the release that threatened to shred his control, and popped his eyes open. Bubbles streamed from his mouth as the air was punched from his lungs. It wasn't the electricity, nor the searing pleasure that did it, but the *sight*.

Floating before him, hands still framing his face, was an unearthly vision.

Hele stared back at him with her eyes of spilled ink. Her long, white hair wove around them like a glowing banner, and her skin shimmered with all the colors of an aurora. The dress, which had been purple, darkened to nearly black — a storm cloud around her hips and thighs against a sky of aquamarine.

He was so arrested by her, by the desire that raked sharp claws across every nerve, that it took him several seconds to realize that Hele was beginning to flounder.

Fuck!

Vael clasped her waist, braced his feet against the smooth floor of the pool, and hauled her up.

Hele sputtered, sparked, and shook her head when they

surfaced. Immediately, her arms snaked around his neck. She pressed her face against his throbbing pulse and whined, "That wasn't *funny!*"

He certainly wasn't laughing. Not when he was about ten seconds and a shock or two away from a mind-shattering orgasm.

Vael wrapped his arms around her lithe form and took several deep breaths. *Control. Calm. Make her feel safe.*

Blinking water out of his eyes, he glanced around the pool. "Gods," he muttered, amazed. "Would you look at that..."

"What?" Her voice was muffled against his wet skin.

He stroked her back as he slowly turned them in a circle. Voice hushed with reverence, he said, "Hele, you make the water *glow.*"

Of course, it always looked a little ethereal, what with the pale blue-green lights he installed around the bottom of the pool and the shimmering, reflective ceiling, but when Hele was in the water, it was something else entirely. Electricity arced over the rippling water, buzzing and snapping, and pops of vivid color bloomed all over the surface.

No wonder I feel like she's rearranging my nervous system, he thought, nearly going cross-eyed when she accidentally pressed her belly against his aching cock. It jerked, throbbing with the beat of his heart. *Gods know what kind of current is running through the water right now. I knew I liked her lightning, but I had no idea it would feel like this.*

He felt her shift, and then her arms tightened. "Is— is this bad?"

"*No.*" Vael cupped the back of her head and exhaled harshly. *Calm.* "No, this is..." If only he were better with fucking *words.* He was humbled by her very presence, by her beauty, by the pleasure of just *being* with her, but he didn't have the damn vocabulary to express it properly.

"Here, let me just show you."

She was like a wet cat, clinging to him with claws and teeth, but he did eventually manage to unwind her arms from around his neck. He didn't want her to stop touching him, but he needed to put some distance between their bodies. *Quickly.* With one hand cupping the back of her head and the other supporting her back, he slowly eased her into a floating position.

Hele's expression was pinched with fear and her hand clutched at his forearm, but she didn't fight him when he began to gently guide her through the water.

"I do not think I'm meant to swim." Her voice trembled.

"Shh. I have you. You're safe. There now," he murmured, watching every minute shift in her expression. "Just relax, *täht.* Breathe for me. Good. Now loosen up— no, you don't have to let go of me. I'm here. Just try to let your muscles relax. That's my good girl."

Hele's eyes were locked on his face for several long minutes, her breathing choppy, but when she finally began to relax, her gaze wandered left and right. Watching her hair fan out around her in the water and the light ripple over her skin...

Vael knew nothing in the world was as magnificent as his mate. *Nothing.*

"That's right," he praised, voice rough as sandpaper, "look around you. See how beautiful you make the water, my Hele. I've never seen anything like it. Good. That's it. Now give a slow kick for me. Yes, perfect. Look at that! You're swimming."

A startled look replaced her wary awe. "I am?"

He grinned down at her. "Yes. See? I'm barely holding you anymore. Just move your arms back and forth while you kick. Slowly."

Chapter Fifteen

Watching Hele discover new things was one of his greatest joys. Seeing her learn to swim, even just a little, was the same.

Slowly, he coached her on floating, then the basics of moving under water. Not all of his knowledge translated well, since he had two extra limbs and a tail with which to move, and she was leery about keeping her head under water for more than a few seconds at a time, but they made it work.

Whenever she learned something new, he rewarded her — and himself — with a slow, drugging kiss. Hele met him enthusiastically. It took willpower he'd never known he had to pry himself away from her again and again. Every time his lust began to cool, it burst to life again, hotter than before.

Eventually, they began to play games. It was mostly to distract himself from the way he felt like he was about to lose his mind, but Hele seemed to enjoy it, too. He playfully chased her around the pool, and he laughed himself to tears when she discovered the honest pleasure of shamelessly splashing an opponent.

His Hele wasn't particularly graceful in the water, especially with her gauzy dress on, but as she became more comfortable, she transformed into the woman he knew — intense, competitive, and eager to play. It was a far cry from the sad creature on the curb, and even farther from the heartbroken mate on the beach.

This was Hele. *His Hele.*

And then, slowly, the playfulness ebbed away. The chase came to a stop and the splash fights ceased. They began to simply twist in slow circles, arms loosely intertwined, and breathe each other's air.

Hele's eyes were half-mast when she whispered, "You did not tell me your story."

Vael breathed deeply and rested his cheek on her damp hair. Sparks nipped at his skin. Each one was a tiny, sizzling kiss. "I don't like to talk about it. It's hard for me."

Soft hands stroked his neck, his shoulders, and the delicate bones of his wings. He shuddered. "I understand. Sometimes I don't want to talk about things. I don't always know how. You don't have to tell me."

He was so damn lucky to have her. Gratitude thrummed through him as he hugged her closer, tighter, until he felt like he could breathe again.

In a hoarse whisper, he said, "I need you to know. I think it'll help you understand why— the reason I was such a dick. Why I thought I was doing the right thing by trying to protect you."

He lifted his head to gauge her expression. Hele stared up at him with her big, dark eyes. In a perfectly solemn voice, she said, "Explain. I will listen."

He did his best. It didn't all come out smoothly, and sometimes he had to pause for an extended period when his throat closed so hard he couldn't get any words out at all.

But he did it.

He told her about his parents, how they had one of those precious, rare triads — two dragons and one prized arrant, his beloved mother, whose earrings he wore every day. His talismans and his reminders.

He told her about his grandparents, all three sets of them, and how they came over from the old country to escape the fury of the Collapse. Like most of the dragons now living in the UTA, his family fled the war that had consumed the dragonlands of the European continent, the complete destruction of hundreds of clans due to civil war and competition for mates.

His grandparents only got a few blessed decades of peace in their new home before war came for them again.

And then he told her about that time, too. How the front crawled toward them as the Packlands dissolved and the elves warred with the orcs. One day he'd woken up to the sound of gunshots and explosions. There was no time to evacuate, not when his grandparents were too weak to fly. They had urged his parents to leave them behind, but they didn't even have time to make that choice.

His fathers, mother, and grandparents died in the shelling. The elves wanted to take a chunk of the 'Riik, hoping to encircle both the Packlands and the Orclind, slowly choking them both, and his family's dwelling lay in their path. Led by Thaddeus II's ruthless shadow Patrol, they swept a bloody tide over the border.

For two days, he lay under the rubble of his home. His wings were shattered, one arm pinned. Fire burned whatever it could reach, and in the narrow gap where he lay, smoke gathered, oily and thick. It would not have bothered another dragon, but Vael was half human, and as a child he was more sensitive, more vulnerable.

The smoke stole his voice before he could work up the courage to scream.

He lay there, shell-shocked and broken, sipping the sweet water that dripped through the cracks in the heavy stone, until Taevas's rogue Wing arrived.

"You know he wasn't always our leader," he explained, soothing himself with a nuzzle against her ear. "For a long time, he was considered a traitor. A rebel. He refused to listen to the old Isand, who thought each dragon should fight for themselves in the traditional way. Taevas didn't believe anyone should be left to defend their roost alone."

Vael did not know what wild, terrible courage it took for a boy of seventeen to become a warlord, uniting clans under his banner even as some of his own people tried to kill him, but he was grateful. He owed Taevas his life. He owed him *everything*.

"He went to every dwelling and searched the rubble himself." Vael closed his eyes, remembering. "He didn't want anyone to be forgotten or discarded. No bodies unclaimed. No orphans left to wander. I'll never forget how he lifted the stone from over my head — how bloody his hand was from digging."

Hele shuddered. Her little fingers curled into the wet strands of his hair and held fast. "I did not know any of this."

"It's not something we like to talk about."

"Yes. I wouldn't want to." Her lips rubbed against the cords of his neck. "But what about your wings? Your injuries?"

He grimaced. "Taevas took me to a field hospital where I was extremely, *extremely* lucky to be cared for by a healer. They put me back together the best they could, but it took years of therapy to fly again. My voice came back faster." He shook his head, half hoping he could rattle those memories loose. "But it didn't matter. I didn't talk for a long, long time. Years. Couldn't think of what to say. What was there to talk about when my clan was gone?"

Hele drew back slowly to look into his eyes. Tentatively, she said, "You did not have a voice."

"No, I didn't." His nose stung with unshed tears when he looked at her tortured expression. Cupping her cheeks, he rasped, "Do you see why it was so important to me that you get every *fucking* opportunity to choose, to live your life? My life was stolen from me. My choices were taken. My future, wiped away. Even knowing that I only ever wanted to give you *everything*, I couldn't stand the thought of taking your choices, Hele. It made me sick to imagine you might regret Choosing me a decade, a century from now, when you could have been doing anything. I had to give you time."

Her fingers trailed down the back of his neck, over the slopes of his shoulders, and down his chest to press against his thundering heart. Water lapped at her knuckles. Her hair, one long banner of white, swirled around them in a graceful arc. "I understand."

He felt something cold and hard snap inside of him — a sudden, violent release of guilt and worry. A tear fell. *"Thank you,"* he whispered.

"You were wrong, though."

A startled, watery laugh bubbled out of him. "Yeah?"

"Yes." Hele leaned forward to peck his nose. "I Chose you because I do not see any future, any choices, without you. This worry that I will feel regret is *just* worry. I won't feel it."

His heart felt too full. Voice breaking, he asked, "Hele, how can you be—"

"Because," she stated simply, "I waited eons for you."

So simple. So sure. Once again, he suspected that his Hele was more dragon than elemental. It was with a dragon's certainty that she stared at him, her chin thrust out and her brow furrowed. It was an expression that said, *I Choose you and there's nothing you can do about it.*

Vael wondered if it was possible to die from relief, from *joy.* Could a heart beat so hard for another that it simply stopped?

He didn't care. If he died from loving his fallen star, then he died the luckiest man on Burden's Earth.

"Eons, huh? Makes my two years look a little less impressive." He pressed a kiss to one corner of her mouth, then the other, before he sipped from her lips again, a little deeper with every leisurely pass. His tail snaked over her hip to hold her tight against him as he slowly walked them back toward the edge. Hele's breath puffed between them in short, excited pants.

Her little nails, blunt like a human's, curled into the tough skin of his chest. "I think you are very impressive."

The sound of her breathless voice made his ego swell —
amongst other things.

Vael groaned when he pressed her back against the wall of the
pool. It forced her chest against his, and when she instinctively
wrapped her legs around his waist, he had to grip the concrete
edge to hold himself still.

"Tell me, *täht,*" he gritted out, his ironclad control over his
baser instincts slipping through his fingers. "Tell me how far this
can go. Tell me what you want."

She blinked owlishly up at him. The look in her eyes was
glassy, her lips parted and swollen. "What I want?"

Had her legs tightened around his hips? He genuinely
couldn't tell if it was his fevered imagination or fact. Either way,
he could feel the heat of her cunt like a fucking brand on the skin
of his stomach. It was *killing* him.

"Sex, Hele." Not elegant and certainly not romantic, but
there it was. Vael pressed his lips against her cheek and rasped,
"Sex. I need to know what you want. What you don't want. Tell
me. You just had your first kiss. I don't want to push you into
something you're not ready for."

"*Oh.*" A beat passed, and then, speaking in that blunt way he
loved so much, she continued, "You push. I will decide if I don't
like it."

"*Hele...*" he warned.

The minx had the audacity to nip his ear! Vael yelped, more
surprised than pained, and pulled back to give her an incredulous
look.

"You will listen to me now!" she demanded, wet hair hissing
with electricity. His mate looked terribly fierce, and he was
dismayed to realize that turned him on even more. "You will
listen, or I will not Choose you again."

Surprise changed its color, shifting into raw, animalistic
possessiveness. He lurched forward again, until they were nose to
nose. The fuse of his instincts lit.

Lifting his lip in a snarl, he said, "Taunt me like that and I'll retaliate, *täht.*"

"Taunt you?" Her black eyes gleamed with heated challenge. "Is it taunting to say I will find another mate who will listen when I say I want him to put his cock in me?"

Vael detonated.

CHAPTER SIXTEEN

HELE WATCHED THE SHREDDED REMAINS OF HER DRESS float away and thought, *Worth it.*

She didn't care that it was once her favorite. What was a dress compared to this moment? Nothing. It was nothing at all.

When Vael cupped her cheeks and kissed her, a low, rumbling growl vibrating in his chest, her thoughts scattered like those scraps of worthless cloth. While she hadn't been entirely sold on kissing at first, she had warmed up to it quickly.

It was so... *tactile.*

She did not think that a being who had the privilege of a body for their entire life could truly comprehend the enormity of touch. At first, even glancing contact had been enough to over-stimulate her nerves, and the idea of seeking out more than the most chaste intimacies had been entirely beyond her.

But over time, she had come to crave new sensations. She learned the difference between a good handshake and bad: eye contact, pressure but not *too* much pressure, one pump, four seconds, release. Alex taught her how to give hugs: move arms with clear intention, steady squeeze, step back with a smile. Her parents guided her with soothing strokes and steady hands:

touches that comforted, that reminded her she was not alone even when it felt like it.

Touch came in so many variations and meanings. What was the difference between *chaste* and *carnal?* What was *comfort* and what was *violence?* How was she supposed to interact with strangers, family, Vael?

There were thousands of nuances in even the simplest touch — and that was before she even considered *copulation.*

Her parents had also gone out of their way to teach her about sex. Dragons weren't shy — not when they could walk around nude at any time — and they did not believe in the concept of blissful ignorance, nor celibacy. A contraceptive that would work with her changing form had been quickly found and her anatomy explained in detail. Her parents had run through the mechanics with her, as well as the concept of firm boundaries. If ever she found herself in a situation where someone touched her without her consent, according to her *isa,* she was supposed to "fry their godsdamned hands off".

They taught her the rules and the facts, but Hele did not understand the true enormity of physical intimacy until Alex introduced her to *novels.*

At night, when everyone else was asleep, she sometimes took breaks from her studying to read about sex and love and drama. It was in books that she discovered her sexuality, strange though it felt, and the budding yearning that drew her to Vael.

Hele knew all about the types of kisses to be had, the creative ways sex could be enjoyed. She knew what a cock did and what an orgasm was supposed to feel like.

But *knowing* something and *experiencing* it were worlds apart.

Reading books did not prepare her for the pleasure of his taste — slightly sweet, with an earthy edge she couldn't put her finger on — nor the way her body felt like something alien when he touched it.

Heat flowed through her veins. Pressure built. Tingles rushed down her spine.

She'd felt *twinges* before, particularly when she watched Vael train, or whenever she caught a whiff of that spicy scent he carried, but it never felt like this — as if she might combust if he didn't touch her. Touching him would work too, if only he didn't have her pinned to the side of the pool, her head held still for his pleasure.

His tongue brushed against hers, wet and silky, while his claws slid into her hair to scratch her scalp. Hele could only make soft sounds of *need* as she stroked his chest, his stomach. Still, he did nothing to ease the ache that built and built between her thighs. Following instinct, she ground herself against his stomach.

Oh!

Hele jolted, amazed and a little wary of the instant, fizzy pleasure that one motion created. She'd experimented with touching herself, of course, but it never felt like *that*.

Vael tore his mouth away from hers. Her head dropped back, her neck suddenly unable to support it, as he arched his spine. She watched him from under her lashes as he peered down at the water between them. The look on his face was harsh, the hard edges of his features pulled into sharp relief as he gnashed his fangs.

"This is killing me," he ground out.

One hand dropped from her hair to slip under water. She felt his tail coil around her ankle in the same moment that his palm met her waist. His whole body moved in a wave as he rolled against the juncture of her thighs. Hot flesh slid against her backside as his pelvis ground them together. Tingles turned into a burst of pleasure.

"Ah!" Hele's back arched. Hair-thin streaks of electricity burst from her skin to shower the water.

Vael's grip tightened to the point of near-pain as his eyes squeezed shut. His hips moved in quick, rolling thrusts. Each one made her gasp. More electricity flew.

All the muscles and cords of his body pulled taut, and then he barked a short, sharp sound. It echoed off of the walls and concrete floor. After several seconds, his erratic thrusts slowed. When he finally opened his eyes, his chest heaved and his wings twitched violently in the water behind him.

Hele arched again, her blunt nails digging into the dense muscle of his abdomen, and whined, "Touch me more. Vael, I *need* it."

Panting, he replied, "I know, *täht.* I just need a minute to catch my breath."

"Why?"

A puff of air exploded from between his lips. It was not quite a laugh, but close. "Because, my Hele, you just made me come."

Hele's eyes opened wide. Glancing between them, she was disappointed to see only the rippling image of her core pressed against the smooth skin of his abdomen. She tried to twist, her head craning to get a look behind her, thinking that it might give her a view of his cock. "I did? How? Can I do it again? I want to see this time."

"Gods give me strength." Vael shook his head hard, a pained look on his face. In a louder voice, he promised, "You'll see it, *täht.* Soon. But first I want to see *you. "*

Before she could argue, both hands clasped her waist and hauled her up. Even the warm air of the room felt cool against her wet skin when he settled her on the edge. Water slid down her skin to gather in her dips and hollows. The droplets tickled, but were quickly forgotten when Vael stepped between her legs and cupped her breasts in his dark hands.

"You have no idea how many times I've imagined this." His gaze was heavy-lidded and intent on her breasts. Slowly, he rolled her dark purple nipples between his fingers, pinching gently.

The breath escaped her lungs with a soft *puh* sound. The swooping feeling she experienced when she dematerialized— that was all she could compare this to, though it was woefully inadequate. Flying did not come with that sweet, insistent pressure, nor the ache that pounded between her thighs. It didn't make her want to squirm, nor to clutch him closer, to *beg.*

She didn't know what to do, so she could only follow her instincts. Shameless, without a hint of modesty or self-consciousness, Hele braced her palms on the edge of the pool, parted her legs, and thrust her chest forward, into his hands. "More, my mate," she demanded, throaty and wild. "Touch me more."

Vael pressed his mouth against the soft flesh of her stomach and groaned. "Again. Call me that again."

A heady sense of power crept over her as she watched his wings tremble, the great span of his shoulders tense. *"My mate,* touch me. Now."

Another groan, this time accompanied by the hot swipe of his tongue over her skin, around her belly button, and down, down toward her cunt. His palms slid up her legs to press against the inside of her thighs, parting them until her heels were braced against the edge of the pool. She watched his tail snake out of the water to curl around her waist. It was a comforting weight, holding her there like he feared she was going to dematerialize at any moment.

Hele was willing to grant that the fear wasn't *unfounded,* but if he asked her, she would have told him that there was nothing in this world that could have compelled her to leave.

Nerves fluttered in her stomach as his hot breath puffed against her wet skin, but they were the buzzy, excited type born of anticipation rather than fear. Hele tracked his every movement with a rapt gaze, unwilling to miss a single second as he traced the seam of her sex with the pads of his fingers.

He choked out a curse, then, gruffly, "Tell me to stop if it's too much."

"I always speak my mind," she primly informed him. "So I will tell you if you do it badly."

His eyes crinkled just before he gave the soft flesh of her inner thigh a quick bite. She gasped, shocked and aroused by the feeling of his fangs nipping her skin. Sounding almost like he was angry with her, he muttered into her flesh, "Gods, I fucking *love* you."

"I—"

Hele didn't finish the thought. It was knocked aside by Vael's fingers, which had reverently parted her, and his long tongue, which swept over her clitoris with aching slowness. Her arms trembled with the effort of keeping her upright.

This is... I do not know the words for this.

The feeling was utterly incomparable to anything she had experienced. It was shivery. Warm. Shocking. Natural. Too much. Not enough. Delicious. *Necessary,* but also unfulfilling.

Her muscles clenched with every slow drag of his tongue. Her breath sped up until her chest sawed up and down. Lights flashed — the electric current of her skin pulsing in time with the rhythmic spasming of her core. The salty scent of the pool and the haze of water in the air filled her head. It gave the moment a bizarre dream-like quality she had never experienced before.

She'd never really considered the tongue an erotic body part, but when Vael slid his down and speared her with it, Hele decided that it might just be her *favorite.*

Keening sounds left her throat and bounced around the room as he curled that wicked tongue inside of her, pressing upward to massage her inner wall. One hand was on her breast, teasing her aching nipple, and the other slowly ground circles around her clitoris. The pressure mounted.

Hele's head fell back. She stared at the reflective ceiling, watching as he licked her, his powerful body bent in worship, and felt her muscles begin to tighten.

"Vael!" She wasn't sure what she was supposed to do as the precipice drew closer, closer. The feeling was raw, bordering on pain. She couldn't decide if she wanted it to stop or go on forever. It was too much. Sensory overload, hideously familiar to her, began to tighten its hold on her.

Just when she was about to panic, the hand on her breast moved upward to grasp her chin. Vael directed her gaze down to him. They locked eyes. She felt the slow, soothing drag of his thumb over the corner of her jaw even as he picked up the speed of his stroking tongue, his grinding fingers.

Stillness.

That's what she felt in that suspended moment, when they stared at one another and unimaginable pleasure hung on a string just out of her reach. Everything was still and sweet and *right*.

And then the string snapped.

Hele couldn't breathe. Her muscles seized and her legs snapped around his ears. She felt his horns digging into the tender skin there, but hardly cared as golden ripples of pleasure washed over her again and again.

His touches gentled, slowed down, but they didn't stop. He guided her through the new and bewildering sensations of her first orgasm — catching her as she fell.

It felt like hours later that her muscles unlocked. Hele sagged back onto her elbows and relaxed her legs. They hung limply over his shoulders, allowing her heels to rest between the base of his impressive wings.

Gentle hands moved her legs back to the edge of the pool. Warm water lapped at her knees as Vael's hot breath puffed against her skin. He skimmed his mouth up over her sex, then her stomach, to press a kiss between her breasts. His hands cupped her back and she gladly let him take her weight as she sagged, utterly boneless.

"You said I'm your mate," he murmured against her throat. She didn't always do well with the nuance of tone or expression, but she was fairly certain he sounded *smug*.

Wrapping her arms around his neck, Hele dreamily replied, "Well, you *did* say you built me a library."

Chapter Seventeen

Vael leaned against the door jamb and crossed his arms over his chest. His gaze was heavy-lidded but focused as it tracked his mate through the little library he'd built for her. Her long, pale legs stretched out from beneath the hem of one of his shirts. Whenever she reached for a book, the slits in the back would flash a tantalizing glimpse of her bare skin.

After Hele recovered from their interlude in the pool, she had demanded to see her library. He was happy to oblige, of course, but he worried about her delicate skin's reaction to the salty pool water, so he'd coaxed her into a quick shower first. It did something to him when she didn't think twice about snagging one of his shirts to wear after the fact — like this was something they'd done a thousand times. It was a sweet glimpse of their future.

It made his chest swell with pride, seeing her in their dwelling, wearing his clothes, but it also made him crave her again. Vael thought that having a taste of her would help calm his instincts down, but it had only made everything worse.

He watched her walk around, looking soft and rumpled, and wanted nothing more than to hoist her up against the shelves, throw her legs over his shoulders, and devour her again.

Lust, momentarily banked after their time in the pool, flared again.

"...organized?"

He shook his head. *Thank fuck I put on pants.* "Sorry, I was distracted. What were you saying?"

Hele had her fingers curled around the edge of one shelf. She was stretched onto her tiptoes, and when she peered over her shoulder at him, Vael's breath caught. *Never seen anything more beautiful than my mate. Especially when she looks like she's fresh from our nest.*

Hele wrinkled her nose at him and replied, "How did you organize the shelves?"

"Ah." He scuffed his foot on the hardwood floor and answered sheepishly, "Can't say I did much organizing. I wasn't sure how you'd want it done, so I just kind of put them on the shelves."

Looking around the long room that had once been the formal dining area, he couldn't help but feel a tiny bit embarrassed. The shelves could only graciously be considered half filled and the two plush chairs at the far end of the room looked strange without a side table or lamp. The library was not even close to being done yet, and a part of him regretted boasting about it now that she was there.

The back of his neck heated. *Damn. I definitely should have waited to show her.*

Shifting uneasily, he apologized, "I'm sorry it's not finished yet. I thought I had more time." He gestured to the chairs. "I am going to get you a nice rug and blankets so your feet don't get cold when you read, and I want to fill all the shelves. I *will.*"

Hele dropped back down onto her heels and turned to pad over to him. "Why are you sorry? You built me a *library.* Now we will fill it together. This is better."

It was automatic, the way his hands reached out to cup her waist, pulling her in until her chest pressed against his. "I just want everything to be perfect for you."

She wrinkled her nose again. "I do not want perfect."

Affection made his chest feel too tight. Being near Hele, feeling her hands on his chest, it was almost too much for him to bear. His joy was immense. Could he hold it all? Vael wasn't sure. He hadn't felt so content in his adult life, and a part of him didn't know what to do with it.

Burying his face in her silky hair, he whispered, "*You* are perfect. I need you to see how in awe I am of you — in everything I do. When I give you something, it has to be worthy of you."

She was quiet for a moment and then, in a small voice, she said, "I think you are the only person in the world who believes I'm perfect."

"I'm your mate," he replied, hoping she understood everything he struggled to articulate.

Hele sucked in a breath. "You are. I do not think I am perfect. Sometimes I wish I was born differently. It would be easier to be a dragon. But... I do not want to be different if it means I could not be your mate."

His tail curled around her thigh and squeezed. Vael wished he could gut every person who had ever made his Hele feel like an outsider, like she wasn't the wonderful, multifaceted gem that she was. But he couldn't. All he could do was love her and hope that she never regretted Choosing a damaged dragon like him to spend her life with.

Vael's voice was a deep, gravelly rumble when he said, "Never. I would *never* wish you were different. I want you as you are — sparks and all."

"I want you as you are, too — scars and all."

It turns out he *couldn't* hold in all his joy. Vael felt it bubbling out of him, running in a current through his trembling limbs, until it found purchase in his twitchy wings. They arched high, quivering with tension, as he held onto the pounding need to embrace her by the thinnest thread.

She had forbidden him from embracing her, but he was desperate. He *needed* to feel her tucked inside the folds of his sensitive wings. *And we are mates now,* he thought, breathing hard. *Isn't that what she said? Only her mate could embrace her?*

Words tumbled out of him in a rush. "Can I embrace you, my mate? *Please.*"

She nodded twice in quick succession.

Finally. Vael's wings closed around them both, sealing them in a cocoon of flesh and bone, where he could keep her safe from the dangers of the world. The millions of fine nerves in his wings hummed when they brushed her delicate form, each one attuned to every one of her breaths, the beat of her heart, the smallest of involuntary movements. They were as vital to his caring for her as his hands or his eyes, and should there ever be a threat, they would be a barrier between her and danger.

Relief washed through him as his instincts settled. He let out a shuddering breath.

This was right. *This* was where she belonged. It was the slowest, cruelest form of torture to have her so near for so long and yet outside of his reach. One of his vital senses had been starved of her for two years. It was done intentionally and not without significant struggle.

But if he had held her before, if he closed his wings around her lithe frame in a dragon's embrace, he knew that he never would have let her go. His will would have turned to dust.

Now, though, he could hold her as much as he liked. And for that privilege, he would sacrifice anything.

Cradling her cheeks, he gently tilted her head back until she met his eyes in the semi-dark. *"Täht...* I love you. I would follow you anywhere." His throat tightened, making his next words husky with feeling. "Even out of the 'Riik, if that's what you want."

Hele blinked. Brow furrowing, she slowly repeated, "Out of the 'Riik?"

"Alex told me that you were thinking of going to school in the Collective," he explained. "I don't want you to think that because we are mates you can't do that, Hele. I'd rather die than clip your wings."

He watched her lips part. Astonishment slackened her expression for several heartbeats before confusion crept in. "But... you are part of the Wing. You can't leave."

Vael breathed deep, filling his lungs with the scent of her, and then exhaled slowly. He did not answer her right away.

Being in the Isand's Wing was the highest honor a dragon could achieve, but for Vael it was more than a position, more than a military honor. It was the fulfillment of a promise he'd made to himself that day in the rubble, when a bloody purple hand had broken through the stone to save an orphan.

He had dedicated himself to Taevas, the man who had sacrificed so much for his people, for the *world*. Being in the Wing was just a formality. What truly mattered was that he was always there, watching Taevas's back, protecting him, *returning the favor*.

But that was before Hele.

He'd dedicated over a hundred years to Taevas and the 'Riik. Was it time to consider the debt paid? Or did he owe him *more* now that he had a mate — a woman he never would have met if not for his Isand's interference?

Vael couldn't begin to untangle that knot, but what he did know was that his mate came first. His pride, his honor, his loyalty — all of it belonged to her now. So if she needed to go find herself outside of the 'Riik and he could not be without her, then the point was moot. Taevas would find another to fill his position, and no matter how much pain that caused him, he would never regret putting Hele first.

Tracing her cheekbones with the tips of his claws, he finally told her, "For you, I'd step aside."

Hele stared at him with wide eyes. "You can't do that. You *love* being in the Wing."

"I love you more."

Fingers curling into fists on his chest, she shot back, "I do not want you to do this. I will tell the witch that I won't take her offer."

His stomach dropped. *"No,* Hele," he growled. "No. You can't limit yourself because of me, okay? I won't let you."

He loved and hated it when her chin thrust forward like that. It meant she was ready to argue, but it was also when he wanted to kiss her most.

"You do not get to tell me what to do," she challenged, black eyes glinting in the soft light that filtered through his wings. "No one does. If I say I will not go, then I will not go. I don't even know if I *want* to go to the Collective. Maybe I want to do something else."

Frustrated and helplessly in love with her, Vael pressed a hard kiss to the crown of her head. "Like what, *täht?*"

"I have not decided. All I know is what I want *now.*"

Vael ran the tip of his nose over the curve of her forehead and then down, until it touched the sharp point of hers. His whisper sounded overly loud in the warm darkness of his wings. "And what is that?"

Her cool fingers tickled the bare skin of his sides. A faint buzz lingered in their path, leaving a trail of sparking nerves wherever she deigned to stroke him. His wings twitched, arching reflexively as her hands neared their base. "I think right *now* I want to see your nest."

"Our nest," he hoarsely corrected her.

"Yes!"

She wiggled with excitement, her grin huge, and made his chest ache with a fierce sort of affection — and regret. *I was such a fool to deny us this,* he thought. How close had he come to missing out on a moment like that?

Hele nearly slipped from between his fingers. Even if he'd pulled his head out of his ass eventually, he felt a cold certainty that if he'd let her go, she never would have given him another chance. The near-miss was as viscerally upsetting as the idea of her being alone with a strange elf.

He could have lost everything, and this time it would have been his fault.

Do not dwell on what-ifs, he heard his papa say, as clear as if he stood beside him. *Move forward.*

I will, he silently replied. *With her. Always with her.*

Voice thick, Vael whispered, "C'mon, *täht*. Let me show you our nest."

~

The look on Hele's face was priceless — for all of five seconds.

Delight and awe disappeared. Vael watched her expression crumble into sadness with a sort of heaving dread he'd never felt before. Hurrying over to where she stood at the edge of the padded floor that was their wall-to-wall mattress, he rasped, "What's wrong? Do you hate it?"

Her chin wobbled as she tightened her arms around her middle. Even her little toes curled inward, as if she felt the need to make herself smaller. "No."

He couldn't stand it. It gutted him to see her upset on a normal day, but *tonight*, in their nest... it struck something fundamental inside of him. The beginning of a mating was a vulnerable time, but knowing how close he'd come to losing her, Vael felt even more high-strung. Panic burned away that feeling of warm contentment.

Grasping her shoulders, he dragged her to his chest and begged, "Tell me what's wrong. Explain it to me."

Hele curled her arms around his waist and buried her face in his neck. "Embrace me again. I feel better when you do it."

She didn't have to ask him twice. Instantly, his quivering wings snapped around them both.

"Tell me what's wrong," he repeated, breathing the words into the crown of her head. Her hair was flat and lifeless against her back — a sure sign of her mood. He wracked his brain, desperate to pinpoint the reason for her sudden distress. "Do you hate the pillows? What? Is it something I did? Do the tapestries upset you?"

Dragons were partial to all crafts, but they had a particular fondness for clothing and fibercraft. High ceilings were a requirement when you could transform into a sixteen foot tall quadrupedal being, after all. That meant they had lots of wall space. Tapestries were not only handy for decorating plain walls, but helped insulate homes traditionally made out of stone.

In the modern age, they were more of a luxury than a practical necessity. Families gifted tapestries for births, deaths, matings, graduations...

Vael had painstakingly chosen the tapestries that decorated their nest. Some reminded him of his family. A few were simply aesthetically pleasing. He'd even commissioned one: A sweeping, handwoven piece that spanned the length of one wall, it depicted the moment of Hele's embodiment — and the shadow of spread wings, ready to catch her.

Did the sight of it upset her? He knew that her creation was not necessarily pleasant, but he thought that perhaps the moment of their meeting might have inspired some joy.

"No, it is *lovely*," she answered, voice garbled. "I am upset because it's a— I can't imagine a more beautiful nest. I love it. But I'm sad because I won't ever be able to sleep here. You've put so much thought into everything, and it is *wasted* on me."

The tight ball of worry between his shoulders eased. Vael let out a long sigh of relief. Stroking her damp hair, he said, "It is not a waste, *täht.*"

She sniffled. "I wish I could sleep like you."

"I don't."

"Why?"

"Because..." He pulled back just enough to flash her a reassuring smile. "*Because* this is like the pool. You thought you couldn't swim with someone else, but you could. The things that make you different from me are *considerations*, not problems."

Hele blinked. Tears glittered in her lashes, catching the light that filtered through the taut membrane of his wings. "Considerations?"

"You think I didn't take that into account when I built our nest?" He *tsked*. "You shame me, my mate. Of course I thought about the fact that you don't sleep."

"I... What did you do?"

"Let me show you."

Slowly, he unwound his wings from around her — silently promising himself that he would embrace her again very soon. Taking her hand, he led her into the heart of the nest. His tail lashed with excitement as he pointed out the floor level lighting she could activate with a gesture of her hand, the shelves built into the walls meant to keep her books and tablet within easy reach at all times, the blankets he had picked out to complement her coloring, and the tapestry that held pride of place above their nest.

Hele stared at it all with wide eyes. Her fingertips hovered over the threads of the tapestry, tracing the shapes of clouds and stars and his wings with reverence. "Is this *us?*"

Vael pressed the pad of his thumb against the white and pale lavender threads that made up Hele's falling form. Stroking them with the utmost care, he answered, "Yes. I commissioned this last year, after I bought the dwelling."

"Why?"

He shrugged. "Because it was the best day of my life."

"Oh." She blinked. Her long fingers trailed up, over the bumps of overlapping thread, to touch the roughened ridge of his scarred knuckles. Vael looked down at her and found her expression somber, her eyes focused on him. "You are forgiven."

He turned his hand over. Twining their fingers together, he gently tugged until she was once more in the shelter of his arms. "Thank you." He smiled ruefully. "I'm not good with words. I wish I could make a grand speech for you like a hero from one of your books. All I can say is that I can't promise I will never fuck up again in the future, but I love you, and I will always try to do better after I make a mistake."

"If you explain, I will listen," she replied, as succinct as ever. He loved how clear she was. There was no obfuscation with his Hele, no guile. She meant what she said and she said what she meant. A perfect fit for him in every way.

After a brief pause, she gave him a narrow-eyed look and added, "And if *I* explain, *you* will listen."

"Deal."

A dazzling smile broke out across her face. Her eyes darted back to the mass of pillows and blankets beneath their feet — so deep and plush it felt like they were being sucked into the world's most comfortable sand dune.

The air hummed with electricity when she announced, "I want to lay in the nest now. I want to touch all the blankets and see if they are as good as the ones you gave me!"

He laughed and slung his arms around her waist. "Did you like the blankets, then?"

"Yes. I always lay with the green one when I read." She peered down at the lavish nest beneath her feet. After a moment of consideration, she nodded once decisively. "It will look nice with the other blankets, I think."

"That was the plan, my mate."

Vael peppered her face with tiny kisses as he gently laid her in the center of the nest. She spread her arms and legs out in a star, feeling the dragon-grade blankets, the down cushions, and made a slightly exaggerated noise of approval for his benefit. Even knowing she was teasing him, it was the proudest he'd ever felt.

Dropping onto his hands and knees over her, he leaned down until their noses bumped. "What do you think now, my Hele? Still sad?"

Her lips skimmed his. Speaking against his mouth, she answered, "Our nest is the best in the whole world."

It felt like his grin was going to stretch clean off of his face. "Yeah?"

"Yes!" Her knees framed his hips. Pulling him closer with

hands hooked around the back of his neck, she added, "There is only one problem."

"What? Not enough blankets?"

A peal of laughter rang in his ears — delicate and tinkling as rain on a window. "No! It doesn't smell like you!"

"Ah, that's an easy fix." Laughing with her, he wrapped his arms around her middle and twisted, rolling them both over and over in the blankets. She wiggled, skin and hair sparking, and he shimmied with her, happily saturating their blankets in *their* scent. And then Hele kissed him again, and her fingertips stroked his sensitive wings, and laughter melted into lust.

Night bled into morning before Vael finally surrendered to sleep, his mate tucked under his wing with a book in her hand.

Chapter Eighteen

It took him decades to find happiness after the death of his clan. What did it matter when his fathers weren't around to feel it? Where could he find it when his mother did not have breath to laugh? What joy existed when his grandparents couldn't savor it?

For a very long time, what happiness he did feel came with a directly proportional wave of guilt and grief. Time eased the reflexive pain, but it didn't wipe it away completely. He still felt his losses when he triumphed. He thought it might be the same when he finally held Hele under his wing.

He was wrong.

It wasn't simply happiness that warmed him the next morning. Holding his Hele against his chest, waking up to his wing draped over her naked form, feeling her slight movements as she carefully turned pages in the book she was reading — it was *bliss.*

There was no kick-back. No reflexive guilt or grief.

Pure contentment settled over him like a sweet fog. It felt like the part of him that had been missing for so long had finally returned to him. He was once again that boy from before the shelling, the one who chattered endlessly and loved his clan more than anything in the world. He'd done everything he could to honor their memory, but only *now* did he feel like he'd truly done it.

The whisper of pages turning and his mate's soft, even breathing sounded like a song from a home he'd lost. Her warmth was the syrupy sunshine from childhood memories.

She was *home.*

Vael buried his face in her fragrant hair. His tail tightened around her thigh, pulling her a tiny bit closer.

You would love her, he thought, imagining his parents, his grandparents. His mother would have found her intelligence delightful. His fathers would have enjoyed her sass and her thoughtfulness. His grandparents would have found endless entertainment in her conversation and the stories they could tell her. He missed them so much it hurt, but that longing did not temper his bliss — it merely added to its depth.

She's so beautiful and stubborn and intelligent. She'd make you laugh one second and then knock your socks off the next.

Tears prickled, but he squeezed his eyes shut to keep them in.

He hoped his clan was proud of him, wherever they were. He hoped they could see how magnificent his Hele was, how much he loved her, and be proud of what the clan had become — small as it was.

Hele shifted against him. A soft hand found the arm he'd wrapped around her waist. Stroking the contours of his forearm, she whispered, "Are you awake?"

His smile was hidden in her abundant hair. "Yes, *täht.*"

"Oh, good." She squirmed a bit before she managed to turn around. Looking very prim despite the early hour, Hele said, "I realized something while you were sleeping."

"What?" He stroked the backs of his claws down the smooth line of her spine. "Did you realize you don't like my snoring?"

"No, your snoring is tolerable."

He gave her softly curved ass a little pinch. "That was a joke! I do *not* snore."

Hele used her paperback to give him a solid whack on the

meat of his shoulder. "Do you want to hear what I realized or not? And you *do* snore. Just a little."

Vael huffed to cover up his laughter. Snagging the book, he carefully dog-eared the page she was on and then tossed it aside. That done, he removed his wing from over her naked form and flipped onto his back. He took her with him, of course.

Hele squeaked when he arranged her on top of him. Her palms pressed down on his chest and her lean thighs bracketed his hips as she stared at him, their noses bumping. A great fall of white hair was a curtain around their faces.

"Go on," he teased, smoothing his hands up and down her thighs.

She was momentarily distracted by their change in position. Hele straightened a bit and looked down at where she was pressed against him, thighs spread, and no doubt had the same thought he did.

They'd done a lot of things the night before — gods have mercy, he hadn't thought to dream she'd love *licking* him so much — but they'd stopped at penetration. He hadn't wanted to push her so soon and she hadn't pressed for more. *Now*, though, he could see the calculation in her eyes as she took in his semi-hard cock and its proximity to the cunt he planned to spoil every damn day of his life.

But Vael had made a promise to her the night before that he would listen when she wanted to explain something, so he playfully tickled the tips of his claws over her bare belly to get her attention before asking, "Well?"

Hele's eye moved slowly away from his cock. When they met his once more, they were as fathomless as ever, but warm in a way that made his heart ache. "I *realized* that you said you loved me last night, but I didn't."

"Oh, *täht*, that's oka—"

"Hush." She patted his chest, silencing him. "I know that I have a lot to learn still, but I also know that I love you. You make me feel safe and like I'm not going to blow away into the sky again. I love hearing you laugh. I want to fly with you all over the world. I Chose you because I do not want a life without you in it. It matters to me that you know this."

"Ah, my Hele," he rasped, "did you spend all night thinking about telling me that?"

"Yes." She paused. "Well, I also read two books."

Laughter bubbled out of him. Framing her face with his hands, he brought her down for a kiss that was mostly smiles. "I love you, *täht.* I'll follow you wherever you wish to go. Even if that is to the Collective."

He could feel her frown against his lips. *"Minu tuli,* we talked about this. I'm not asking you to give up—"

"My fire?" He kissed her again, more deeply, both to quiet her protests and to express how much he loved the nickname she'd chosen for him. "Why *minu tuli?"*

"Because," she answered, exasperated and breathless, "you were the first warmth I felt. But I don't want to talk about that. I want to talk about—"

"No more talking." He pressed a hot, open-mouthed kiss to her throat, right where her pulse throbbed. When he felt her go soft against him, he whispered, "Your *tuli* wants to show you how much he loves you."

Hele's hands slid down his chest. When he felt the cool flesh of her palm on his shaft, he groaned.

"Fine," she replied, stroking him with maddening slowness. "We will talk *later.*"

His hands found her breasts, perfect and small and made just for him. "Yes. Later."

Much, *much* later.

Gods, her fingers were so soft, but when they made contact with his skin, a ripple of electricity passed between them. It was like having the softest, most gentle current hooked up directly to his cock. He hadn't been able to control himself in the pool — the nerves could only take so much stimulation, after all — but he'd done his best since then to grit his teeth and make it last.

It didn't matter how hard he tried, though. Would anyone be able to resist such sweet torture?

Squeezing her small, pert breasts perhaps a touch too roughly, Vael groaned, "If you do not stop soon, I'll come again."

Hele smiled. Instead of stopping, she cupped him with both hands and slowed her strokes down, each pass a hard, sizzling pull that made his toes curl. "I like to touch you," she said, "and I love to watch you come. I want to learn all the different ways to do it."

Fuck.

Vael's spine stiffened as he fought for breath. He wasn't entirely sure how he, the one with sexual experience, ended up being the one ravished, but he loved it. When Hele handled him, it was with the utmost focus and care. When she looked at him, it was with the kind of desire that made a man feel like something *more.* And when she raised herself up onto her knees to slowly notch his cock at her soft, wet core, it was with the wild-eyed determination to *claim.*

It took an enormous amount of willpower for him to drop his seeking hands from her breasts to her lean hips, stalling her descent. "Hele, are you sure? We don't need to rush. You don't have to—"

"I want to try." She tilted her head to one side, her gaze locked on his face. Her shoulders rose and fell rapidly as she panted. Vael swore he could even feel her inner thighs trembling against his hip bones when she asked, "Do you?"

Involuntarily, he glanced down to where she held him perilously close to paradise. His cock looked huge and lewd against her soft flesh. Leaking pre-come, his skin a dark, livid green, and almost as wide as her dainty wrist, it was a vision of depravity. When she slowly thumbed the flared head and swirled it around her swollen clitoris with a little experimental swivel...

It took him a second to find his tongue again.

"Yes," he growled, slowly pushing her hips back and forth,

encouraging her to use him like she needed. "Yes, *täht*. But we will stop if you don't like it."

Hele's black eyes glittered at him through her long, white lashes. A soft moan built in her throat as she worked his cock against her wet skin, chasing sweet friction. "I will like it."

He wasn't so sure. He was a big bastard, after all, and his Hele was reed thin and as delicate as spun glass. If she'd never experimented with any toys before, he had his doubts that this would be as pleasurable as she hoped.

"Ah-ah, let me prepare you first," he choked out, stopping her again as she made to press herself down. His balls were drawn up tight, his shaft ached like it might fucking explode, and the sight of her *almost* riding him was enough to make him lose his mind, but Vael still somehow managed to slow things down.

Hele made an impatient chuffing sound. "Why?"

"Because you are probably tight as a fucking vice and I don't want to hurt you." He slid his hands down over the tops of her shaking thighs to where they were almost joined. It did something dark and primal to him to feel that — where the hot skin of his cock nearly breached her cunt, so slick and ready for him.

And because he just couldn't fucking help himself, Vael rumbled, "Have you ever put anything in this pretty little pussy before, sweet mate?"

He felt Hele start, as if for once *she* was the one who'd been electrocuted. "Only my fingers," she breathed. "I didn't see the appeal. It felt like nothing."

Sweat dewed on his chest and throat. *Gods help me. I'm going to ruin her.*

"Were you wet when you tried it?"

Hele shook her head. "No. That only happens when I look at you."

If he wasn't so turned on, Vael would have been embarrassed by the way his voice went up an octave when he asked, "What?"

Her hips began to slowly grind again, nearly wedging the head of his cock into that hot, wet core that threatened to steal every ounce of good sense he possessed. Her eyes skimmed over him, taking him in like she just couldn't get enough. Licking her lips, she murmured, "When I look at you, it makes me ache. That's why I go to the Roost when you do your exercises. I like how it feels when I watch you. It's like you're touching me between my thighs even when you're not."

Chapter Nineteen

Vael felt like he was falling into a dark chasm where there was only hot air, the scent of her, and the heavy feeling of her gaze on his skin. He couldn't breathe. He couldn't even see anything besides her. The world was a tiny pinprick of light ahead of him, blazing blue and green and pale purple.

Before Hele, he did not necessarily *lack* sexual partners. A certain kind of woman craved the power in his limbs, the position he held in the Wing. Some simply liked a brutish face and a big cock. It wasn't complicated, and he'd never expected more than that.

He wasn't exactly pretty. He didn't have Artem's boyish charm, nor Taevas's roguish sex appeal. Even Mad Radek was better looking than he was, despite the fact that a hundred and some years of misery had given his face a savage cast.

It didn't bother him too much that he was generally the last man women fluttered their lashes at. He wasn't affable enough to make up for what he lacked in looks, and his size tended to intimidate more than it enticed. His nose was a harsh, broad blade between dark eyes, and his brows were too heavy. A looker he was simply *not*.

So he had never experienced the pure reverence that his mate exuded when she ran her delicate fingers over each dip and hollow of his body. He did not know what to do with her rapt gaze, nor her hungry little sounds.

He was truly *desired*. It was utterly disorienting.

Again, he wondered how the tables had turned and *when*. Wasn't he the one who was supposed to worship? He was the lucky motherfucker with an exquisite, cosmic-entity-made-flesh mate. He was the one with experience. He was the dominant one of their pair.

But... none of that mattered.

Between them, one to one, there was no pretense, no dominance play, no carefully choreographed dance. Pleasure was simply pleasure, and it was taken as easily as it was given. Hele hid nothing — including her unrestrained desire for him.

"There is no man luckier than me," he grated, consumed by the image of her watching him from the lounge areas around the training grounds, her cunt wet and aching for him. *Him.* The ugly orphan with fucked up wings and zero charm.

Vael couldn't restrain a deep, subvocal growl of appreciation as he slid his hand down, fingers slipping over slick skin to find her clitoris. Her grip on his cock tightened reflexively as she rocked into his hand. "I'm going to explain what'll happen next, okay, *täht?*"

"Yes, yes, explain." The pad of her thumb swirled around the tip of his cock, spreading the pearly drops there in a way that might have seemed absentminded if she didn't immediately bring her thumb up to her mouth for a taste.

Her cheeks flushed as she sucked it into her mouth, reminding him of how she looked when she went down on him the previous night. Vael's cock jerked against his flat stomach, so hard and full it felt like his skin was being stretched to its limits. He swore every single drop of blood he possessed was in his shaft.

Hele was *greedy*.

He never would have guessed that, considering how well she had inadvertently concealed her lust, but Vael was rapidly coming to understand that his mate *loved* cock.

Truly I am blessed.

"So fucking good to me," he muttered, petting her cunt with the reverence it deserved. "My *täht,* I'm going to get you ready for my cock. If I tried to fuck you now, you'd be in too much pain to enjoy it at all, so I have to stretch you first."

Hele's thumb slid out of her mouth with a wet *pop!* "Then stretch me."

No hesitation at all. Complete trust. Overwhelming enthusiasm. *Perfect. My Hele is perfect in every godsdamned way.*

"You'll need to hold very still for me," he told her, blood rushing impossibly faster. "I'm going to put my fingers in you, but my claws are sharp, so I have to be extremely careful. You can't move an inch. Understood?"

She nodded twice, quick and eager. Her hair, that ethereal mass of sparking white, drifted upward over her shoulders and head to sizzle in the air. The air in the nest was saturated in the scents of ozone, strawberries, and sex.

"Do I get to watch?"

Vael's fingers jumped, momentarily losing their path to the dripping entrance of her cunt. He groaned. "Yes. Watch me, *täht.*"

That dark, drugging feeling of primal satisfaction ratcheted up a notch when Hele leaned back slightly onto her palms, angling herself so she could peer down to where he slowly rubbed circles around her entrance. She bit her bottom lip and spread her legs wider, her knees digging into the soft blankets and cushions of their nest on either side of his hips.

Vael couldn't stop himself from praising her as he slowly, oh-so-carefully inserted his middle finger into the tight, rippling heat of her core. "You are perfect. So fucking perfect."

More pre-come smeared the skin of his stomach when he felt her inner walls contract around him. Hele gasped, her eyes popping open wide as they locked on the sight of his thick digit sinking into her.

Her whole body quivered when he slowly stroked her from the inside. "That— That does not feel the same as my fingers. Or your tongue."

"You needed more than your fingers could give you, that's all," he explained, beginning to pump shallowly. With his claws as they were, he'd never be able to fuck her with his hand like he wanted to. *Have to trim them. Don't care if they'll be useless in a fight.*

Hele nodded. A quick glance down confirmed that she'd gripped the nest with white-knuckled fists. "Yes. Yes, more."

"My good little mate," he breathed. "I think you're hungry for cock. Is that what you need?"

He watched the muscles of her stomach tense and *felt* the contraction around his finger as his words registered. "I *am.*" Hele's breath exploded in quick pants between words. "I love to touch it. I want it in my mouth. I need it everywhere."

"So greedy." Vael rewarded her honesty by gently working in another finger. There was definitely more resistance that time, and the resulting stretch made Hele tense.

Instinct reared its head. Desperate to soothe, his tail snaked around her waist. The smooth skin of the side of his tail pressed down against her clitoris and slowly sawed back and forth. "Relax," he rumbled, stroking, rubbing, easing the sting in every way he could. "Breathe through it, my mate. Breathe and hold still. Let me open you or you'll never get my cock in here."

He waited until Hele was breathing normally again before he began to build a rhythm — shallow pumps, then a firm massage to that soft spot that made her gasp, followed by a slow scissoring of his fingers. Again and again he did this, until his mate was speaking incoherently and sparks flew from her skin like the smallest lightning bolts.

Sweat dripped down his body to pool in the hollows of his

abdomen and collarbone. His focus was single-minded, but his restraint held on by the thinnest thread. The eroticism of seeing his mate desperately hold herself still as he fucked her with his hand was indescribable.

"Almost there, *täht,*" he told her, voice breaking under the strain of his need. "One more and then you can take me. Relax for me. Breathe— ah, there you go."

A soft whine built in the back of her throat, hammering at his instincts. Her svelte thighs trembled as she squeezed her eyes shut. "I... understand why you worried. This is not pleasant anymore."

"It will ease. I promise it will feel good again in a second." His free hand moved up to cup her jaw. Tilting her head down, he gave it a small squeeze and murmured, "Look at me, my mate."

Hele shuddered. Her eyes cracked open a sliver.

Gently, he withdrew his fingers and then pushed them back in. He watched her expression pinch as the discomfort registered. He hated that look.

Vael lived for her comfort. He despised her pain even when it preluded pleasure. There were many people who loved a bite of discomfort with their sex, but he wasn't one of them. He didn't know many dragons who did.

They were hardwired to spoil, both biologically and culturally. A mate's pleasure was as sacred as their place in the nest. Did that mean the same thing for everyone? No, of course not. But most dragons he knew would prefer to watch their bed partners cry from too *much* pleasure than too little.

Vael suspected that was why they had such a positive attitude toward sex in general. Ignorance benefitted no one, and the ridiculous worship of virginity led to discomfort and shame. While Vael treasured the idea of being his mate's *only* in a very primal sense, there was a small part of him that loathed this process.

"You are doing so well," he assured her. "Look at me, *täht*. Do you even know how much I love to watch you discover new things? You are so brave. Always looking to learn something new, even when it scares you. This is no different."

Hele watched him with an unblinking stare, her breath held. He withdrew. Pushed in. Fluttered the pads of his fingers against her inner wall. Repeated the process. All the while, he dredged up words for her, ones he had saved for two years — all the ways he adored her, how beautiful she was, how sweet she tasted, the dreams he had for them, the fantasies she had already fulfilled.

He caught the moment discomfort shifted back into pleasure. Hot, wet sounds accompanied each push and pull of his fingers, as well as the slow, determined sliding of his tail. Her inner walls began to flutter.

"*Minu tuli!*" she gasped, stiffening until her whole body went rigid above him.

Electricity thickened the air and snapped across his skin as she came. Vael gritted his teeth and coaxed her through it, milking the orgasm for all it was worth until she went lax, her shoulders slumping as she caught her weight on her locked arms.

His tail stayed in place as he skimmed his hands over her stomach to cup her little breasts. Circling her tight nipples with the pads of his thumbs, he gently drew her attention back to him.

"How do you feel, *täht?*"

Hele stared at him with a blissed out expression. "Relaxed."

He held in a laugh. *That makes one of us.* Vael felt like he was half a second from coming out of his skin when he asked, "Did you still want to try? We don't have to—"

He didn't get to finish the sentence.

Hele's hand was on his cock instantly, almost as fast as her damn lightning. Vael jumped, nerves firing, and tossed back his head with a small shout when she gave it a firm squeeze.

"I want to know this," she told him, using that familiar stubborn tone that both delighted and vexed him. The heat of her core kissed the head of his cock as she levered herself up and notched him at her entrance once more.

"Slow, Hele. Slow," he choked out. To steady himself, he grasped her waist, but his hands shook too badly to truly help.

And then she sank down.

They let out simultaneous exclamations. Vael's was a bark of disbelief, of pleasure so acute it blotted out everything else, and Hele's was one of surprise. It was more of a yelp, really.

Her hands slapped down on his chest as she held herself perfectly still, his cock only a quarter of the way in. She sucked in huge lungfuls of air as she struggled to take him. Desperate to help her and himself, Vael managed to wheeze out, "Easy. Easy. Just— just hold yourself there for a moment. Breathe through it. Then slowly drop down."

Blunt nails bit into his pecs. Cracking open his eyes, Vael found his mate staring at him with a look of such ferocious determination, it made the hair on the back of his neck rise.

"I do not like slow," she hissed, bracing herself.

"Hele, *no—*"

She dropped her weight down. His cock slid home in one quick, glorious glide.

Vael had sex with relative frequency before he met Hele. Was he the most popular dragon around? No, but they were lusty creatures on the whole, so he could find a partner when the need struck him. He *knew* what sex was — good and bad.

No experience could have possibly prepared him for Hele.

Her cunt was as hot as a brand, tight enough to border on uncomfortable, and *buzzed* with a subtle electricity that only the hyper-sensitive nerves of his cock could detect.

"Fuck!" Vael's back arched. His wings, spread out beneath him, shot out to span the entire width of the nest. Pillows and blankets scattered. All his tendons were pulled taut and every muscle shook with the sudden strain of keeping his orgasm at bay.

His heart jackknifed in his chest. *I'm going to die. She's going to kill me. Gods, I am so fucking lucky.*

He somehow managed to lift his head. "Hele," he gasped. "Hele, are you all right?"

She took a moment to answer, but when she did, her voice was strong, if not necessarily *pleased*. "Yes. Tell me— tell me what to do now. Explain."

"Of course, *täht*. Just give me a minute. It feels like you're squeezing me with a fucking fist and electrocuting me at the same time."

He felt her tense. A wavering note of uncertainty accompanied a flex of her fingers on his chest. "Is that bad? Did I do it wrong?"

"Aw, fuck, no. No." Vael tried to find *words*. He was shit with them on a good day, but the feeling of his mate's cunt seemed to have completely scattered whatever he had left.

But even if he was a good talker, how the fuck could he describe *this?* There was nothing like it. There was nothing better. Any words he could have had would have done a disservice to the pleasure that ran like molten fire through his veins and the vision she made, impaled on him, hair waving around her like slow motion lightning.

Shuddering, he dared to skim his right hand down, past where his rigid tail was pressed against her like it was terrified to move, to flutter the pads of his fingers around where they were joined. He let out a guttural groan of pleasure — and then another one when Hele responded by clenching around him.

"You're perfect," he gasped out, greedily tracing the seam where her flesh wrapped around his again and again. "So fucking perfect. I promise. Just— *Täht,* there isn't a science to this. Move when you feel comfortable. Find what feels good. I *promise* I'll love whatever you do."

She put more pressure on his chest as Hele leaned forward to stare down at him, her eyes bright and her cheeks flushed. "Can I make you come like this?"

Vael's hips jerked involuntarily. "Gods, *yes.*"

"Good. I want to see it."

Hele sat back on her knees again and, gods help him, started to *move*.

Like their time in the pool, she started out a little clumsy, her rhythm stuttering, before she eventually found a pace and a position that suited her. Vael could only hold on for dear life as she rode him hard. Eventually their fingers intertwined, and Hele began to use her grip for leverage.

Wet sounds of flesh meeting flesh filled the nest, and although he was determined to hold out, to let her use him until she had what she needed, Vael couldn't be entirely passive. His hips rolled up to meet her and his tail strummed her clitoris, stroking back and forth, back and forth, until she began to stiffen again.

The pressure was almost too much. Vael chased his orgasm as hers began to crest, his hips pistoning up and down with more power than finesse. Worrying that she would simply bounce off if she didn't hold on, he untangled their fingers to clasp her nape. He dragged her down, forcing her weight onto her palms by his ears, and sucked her tongue into his mouth as he finally came.

It took them both a while to come down. He panted against her lips as the stars finally began to clear from his eyes.

Hele's mouth formed a soft moue. A quiet sound of discontent escaped her, piercing the haze of his orgasm.

Pulling back to look her in the eye, he asked, "What? What's wrong? Are you in pain?"

Her brow crinkled and her lower lip thrust out. "No."

Relief came with confusion. He stroked strands of white hair back from her damp forehead. "Then why the face, my mate? I thought we did pretty damn good."

"It was good," she agreed, tilting her head into his hand. "But I didn't get to see you come. *Again.*"

Vael gasped out a husky laugh. "Ah, my greedy mate. We have plenty of time to try again."

Her pale brows lifted. "You're right." He felt her slowly, *deliberately* clench around his softening cock. "We will try again."

"*Now?*"

Those black eyes, as dark and deep as the space between stars, stared down at him with a wicked sort of hunger. "Yes, now. I want to know *everything.*"

Vael groaned. Flipping her over so that she lay sprawled on the nest below him, he rasped against her lips, "I am *so* fucking lucky."

CHAPTER TWENTY

THEY SPENT THREE DAYS TOGETHER IN THE NEST. VAEL couldn't remember the last time he'd rested so thoroughly or had so much fun as he did with his Chosen.

They watched entertainment feeds, splashed in the pool, and when she got restless, they flew together. He loved flying with her, and not just because she'd discovered that she could toy with him mid-flight when he was in his bipedal form. For reasons that both baffled and delighted him, she was determined to see if she could coax him into making love *mid-air*.

Hele thought it was a grand game, and the more he disagreed with her, the more determined she became. This resulted in more than a few spontaneous materializations mid-air, forcing him to catch her and give her sneaky hands ample opportunity to wander while he tried to keep them from falling to their deaths even as he laughed.

Vael couldn't honestly say he minded, since it usually ended with them landing somewhere remote and ravishing one another. He didn't think he could ever complain about how greedy his little mate was for him.

If he'd ever had any doubts about them, they would have evaporated after day one. They laughed constantly, even when they bickered. He loved waking up to her in his arms and listening to her tell him everything she'd thought of while he slept. He couldn't imagine not watching her delicately nibble on fruit as they both lay naked and exhausted in the nest, her rare hunger roused by an orgasm or three, or feeling her next to him, content with a book, as he watched sports feeds.

He hadn't taken time off in… ever, but as his five days away from his duties drew to a close, Vael understood that his life was now entirely different. Things had to change.

They hadn't spoken much more about her opportunity in the Collective mostly because he did everything he could to avoid it. Whenever it did come up, neither would give an inch, leaving the argument in a permanent stalemate until finally he informed her that he intended to resign whether she agreed or not.

Hele had given him the silent treatment for all of two hours before she admitted, in her blunt way, *"You did not want me to hate you for Choosing too soon. I am worried you will hate me for giving up something so important."*

"My Hele," he had whispered, *"you are the most important thing in my life now. You will just have to trust me when I say this is the right thing to do."*

Vael had served his Isand for over one hundred years. It hurt to give that place up, but for Hele, it was worth it.

For his Chosen, a dragon would do *anything*.

So on the final day of his forced vacation, he encouraged Hele to meet with the witches again. They had sent her a number of follow-up questions after their first meeting, and he had watched his mate glow with enthusiasm as she answered them.

Even if she did not choose to go to school in the Collective, she belonged in their world, making a difference, and he flatly refused to hold her back. To give her what she deserved, his whole life could no longer revolve around his incredibly time-consuming duties. It had to revolve around *them*.

He loved being in the Wing, but after a stretch of uninterrupted days with her, he knew that he loved being with her more.

Hele knew he intended to resign, but she didn't know when. He preferred it that way. His mate would worry, and if he could avoid that, he would. While he felt guilty for not telling her what he planned to do, Vael knew that it was necessary. His mate would forgive him.

Eventually.

After dropping her off at the research facility just after it opened for the day, Vael went directly to the Roost — Taevas's home and the center of the 'Riik's government.

The architecture of Drummond Island's Roost was starkly beautiful and sky-high. A hive of stone and latticework, it was a fortress guarded not only by a net of wards and advanced security equipment, but the barracks of dragons and other beings who made up the highest levels of the military.

It was not the only capital — Manhattan was their secondary Roost and financial center, of course, as well as where the Isand stayed several months out of the year — but it was their *home.*

Most importantly, it was *Taevas's* roost.

His dwelling towered over the hive. It was a spire of black glass and smooth, polished stone; at once ancient and new, embracing tradition even as it integrated the modern. An elegantly wrought dagger that sliced through the dome of the sky, as sharp and hard as the Isand himself.

Vael was one of the few who had blanket permission to land on the Isand's perch. His tattoos were not just the symbols of rank, nor designed to identify his body in case of the worst, but sigils that allowed him through the choking web of wards that kept the Isand and the rest of the island secure.

He landed on the wide perch and stood there for a moment, scanning the massive wall of windows that spanned the entire floor. He knew that Taevas would sense him there and would be out when it suited him.

Shoving his hands into the pockets of his jeans, Vael fought to keep his wings from betraying his nerves. The brisk wind ruffled his hair and a sour taste lingered on the back of his tongue. Not because of bitterness, but because of worry.

This was right. He had to give his mate time to live her life. He didn't resent that. But what would happen to Taevas when he wasn't there to watch his back? The other members of the Wing would keep him safe. He knew that. But Vael owed Taevas his life, and that was not a burden easily shed.

And more than that, he wondered who *he* would be, if not the shadow of the Isand? Vael didn't have any answers there, only the conviction that he was doing the right thing for the tiny clan that owned him, heart and soul.

Movement drew his eye back to the windows. The familiar, broad shouldered shape of his Isand stood just on the other side, a cup of coffee in one hand. The other raised and, with a lazy flick of a wrist, welcomed Vael inside.

He'd been to the Isand's roost hundreds of times over the years. He'd even crashed there once or twice after a long, exhausting trip or a few too many drinks. The grandeur still hit him every time he saw it.

The interior of Taevas's home was all black marble, dark wood, and leather. Every surface was polished, and the sitting room he stepped into was vast. A sleek bar spanned one side of the room and a sunken living space took the other. It was big enough to fit at least two dozen people — though Taevas only ever hosted family and members of the Wing, and never anywhere but in that room.

Their Isand shared much with the world — his time, his energy, his love, even his *blood* — but when it came to his roost, he was deeply private.

As it should be, Vael thought, stepping over to the bar to make himself a cup of coffee like he had a thousand times. *The nest is sacred. If he should keep anything to himself, it's that.*

"So," Taevas drawled, "I hear you owe Alex a cellphone."

Vael looked up from the machine to find his Isand leaning against the bar, his long black hair slightly damp and his white dress shirt partially unbuttoned. Like everything else he wore, it was liberally dotted with rich embroidery around the cuffs and collar. Today, sprigs of what appeared to be olive leaves curled against the white fabric in pale blue-greens and browns.

It didn't take a dragon's keen eye to notice that it was craftsmanship of the finest quality, nor that it was imbued with a humming power — an extra layer of magical protection that had to cost the Isand many thousands of dollars per garment.

It was always a relief to see Taevas in his rich embroidery, though Vael did sometimes wonder about his taste in design.

Clearing his throat, Vael looked back at his mug just in time to see the last steaming drops of his coffee splash. "Yep," he answered gruffly.

"Uh-huh." He felt Taevas's eyes on him as they both took long sips of their coffee. "Do I get to know why?"

"Sure." Vael eyeballed his Isand from over the rim of his mug, weighing his words with cold-hearted calculation. "Alex set Hele up on a date with a junior member of the EVP's embassy staff named *Jacques du Soleil.*"

Taevas took another sip. Maintaining steady eye-contact, he asked, "And is Jacques du Soleil alive?"

"Yes."

"Interesting. Why?"

Vael had to work very hard to keep his voice level when he answered, "Because he wasn't there when I tracked her down. He ditched her."

"Ah." Another sip, then, pleasantly, "Looks like I'll be having a word with Mr. du Soleil this afternoon."

"Thought you might want to handle that."

"Yes," Taevas replied, smiling wryly, "I suppose it is less of a mess than if I'd had to text dear little Teddy *'sorry, one of my men tore your diplomat limb from limb'.*"

"I was fucking tempted."

"Rightfully so. Little prick is lucky *I* don't plan on roasting him alive." Taevas's normally faintly amused expression hardened, revealing the man underneath the mask: a ruthless predator who would and *had* done anything to protect those in his care.

"My bet is he didn't realize my mate is an Aždaja."

"Then he's not just a prick, he's a *stupid* prick." Taevas grimaced. His fangs flashed in the morning sunlight that streamed in from the floor to ceiling windows. "I would have broken Alex's phone, too. What the fuck was she thinking?"

"She wanted me to pull my head out of my ass." Vael shrugged and peered down at the steaming pool of coffee in his earthenware mug. "It worked, obviously. I didn't *mean* to break her phone, though. That was an accident."

Visibly reining in his temper, Taevas shook out his massive, purple wings and took another long sip of his coffee. When he lifted his arm, Vael spied more sprigs of olive leaves around the slit in the wrist cuff. It looked like the leaves were falling down his forearms to pool around his wrists. A rather subdued design for a man who was known for wearing velvet suits, leather, and gold.

"Well then, I suppose I should be congratulating you and my cousin," his Isand said, tipping his mug in a salute. "I assume you've Chosen one another, what with the head-ass removal?"

This moment might have made him puff with pride and maybe even a little self-deprecating laughter if Vael didn't feel a bit like throwing up. "Yes," he answered, setting his coffee down on the bar. Elation warred with the dread of what he had to do. "I don't know *why* she Chose me, but she did. I'm so fucking lucky."

Taevas snorted. "Eh, no accounting for taste."

"Shut up." Vael wadded up a small stack of cocktail napkins that sat next to the coffee maker and tossed them at his Isand. Without so much as a glance, Taevas's long purple tail snapped out to intercept it, sending the paper ball across the room.

"It's about damn time." He eyeballed Vael with barely concealed reproach. "She's been mooning after you for over a year. I was starting to get annoyed with you on her behalf."

"I was *trying* to give her time."

Taevas snorted. "Keep giving someone a gift they don't want and eventually they're going to bust your ass about it."

Vael rubbed the back of his neck and grimaced. "I was an idiot. I should have been looking for the signs and listening when she told me what she needed. I was just trying to take care of her."

"You're not the first dragon to think with his instincts rather than his brain," Taevas sagely replied.

"You never have that issue." Vael shook his head, even more impressed with his Isand's coolheadedness than he usually was. He'd never *once* seen Taevas give in to his baser instincts — for a woman or anything else. He was playful, yes, but also tightly controlled.

"I don't, but then again, I am not exactly a normal dragon." His Isand's lips twisted, not into their usual smirk, but into a wry, close-lipped smile. Tilting his mug in Vael's direction, he continued, "But this discussion is not about me. It's about you, and how you came here to forfeit your place in the Wing."

Vael jolted. His heart beat double time in his chest when he rasped, "What? How do you—"

"Because I know you," Taevas answered. "We've only spent over a hundred years together. It happens."

Words failed him. Vael could only stare at him, his chest aching with the expanding pressure of conflicted guilt and stalwart conviction. After several strained seconds, all he could manage was, "I..."

Taevas swallowed a sip of his coffee before he snorted. "Don't give me that look, whelp. I never said I was *accepting* your resignation."

Vael's brow furrowed. "Wait, what? You can't do that."

It was Taevas's turn to throw something. Snagging a lime from a stainless steel bowl just behind the bar, he tossed it at Vael's head. It bounced off of a horn before it landed somewhere on the marble floor behind him.

"I can do whatever I fucking want," Taevas informed him,

brows arched in challenge. "If I say you aren't quitting, then you aren't quitting. I'm your Isand. I make the fucking rules."

Indignation began to bleed through his astonishment. The desire to care for his mate in the way she needed made him less inclined to let Taevas bulldoze his will. "No, not in this. Hele needs the freedom to find herself, and I can't give her that when I'm chained to the duties of the Wing. And since I can't exactly reduce the load, then I *have* to quit." His voice broke. "I know that I'm letting you down, but my mate needs—"

"It's like you've learned nothing from this spat with Hele." Taevas rolled his eyes. "You aren't listening to me, Vael. I'm telling you that you aren't quitting because you don't *have* to."

Vael speared his claws into his short hair and tugged. "I don't understand."

Taevas plonked his mug onto the bartop. The humor disappeared from his expression in an instant. "Vael, you have served the 'Riik and me since you were barely more than a kid. *Every single day* of your life, you've served. I allowed it because I thought it gave you purpose and the sense of having a clan again, but I draw the fucking line at you thinking that you are failing me or the 'Riik by taking *time off.*"

Taevas circled the bar to stand in front of him. Dropping a heavy hand onto his shoulder, he leaned in and rumbled, "You are not letting me down. You got it into your head when you were a kid that you owed me something for digging you out of that rubble, but you didn't and you don't. And even if you did, that debt would have been paid a thousand times over by now."

Vael's throat tightened painfully. He couldn't bear to look at his Isand, so instead he closed his eyes and lowered his head until his forehead touched the crisp fabric pulled tight over Taevas's broad shoulder. All he could manage to croak was, "You saved me."

"And you have watched my back every day since you were a teenager. We're fucking even." Strong, clawed fingers glittering with gold bands squeezed his shoulder. "You're taking a sabbatical. Go live your life with my cousin. Have fun. Raise some little electric dragons while she gets her PhD or whatever. Let her run you ragged. This doesn't have to be a sacrifice for Hele. It can be about finding out who you are as well."

Taevas's hand moved to the nape of his neck. Grasping it with playful roughness, he continued, "And when you're ready to come home, your position will be waiting for you. Maybe you won't want it, or maybe you'll need to make changes to your duties. What-fucking-ever. You've more than earned a permanent space in the Wing, Vael. That's not going to change. Those tattoos aren't exactly temporary, are they?"

The spiky ball of dread that he had been carrying in his chest deflated in a rush. Vael shuddered, unspeakably relieved.

It was a fact that joining the Wing, watching Taevas's back, had given him what he needed after his family was destroyed. It was also true that Vael didn't rightly know who he was *outside* of the Wing.

He understood that he needed to abandon his duties for Hele, but it was only then, standing in Taevas's great shadow, that he realized how much he needed to do it for himself, too.

The prospect of spending so much time with his Hele, building something good and solid with her, as they both discovered themselves in the world was enough to make tears prickle behind his eyes. There would be no pressure. No rush. Just *them*.

And when they were ready, he could resume his duties and Hele could do whatever it was that pleased her. Or not. The future was open and full of possibility.

A watery laugh burst out of him. "Thank you, Taevas."

"Yeah, yeah." He pulled back with his signature wry grin. Slapping Vael's shoulder, he said, "You should go tell the rest of the jokers. Before you go, I'll have you help me pick out who should take your place in the rotation. I have some ideas, but I want your input."

Pride was a warm glow. It prickled every nerve and made him wish that Hele was there. He wanted nothing more than to clasp her to his chest, to bask in her and the feeling that everything was okay.

"You're right," he answered, wiping his eyes. "I'll go tell them now."

Taevas gave him a playful shove toward the glass doors. "Go on then. You'll want to tell your mate, too, I suspect."

Vael grimaced. "Ah, yes. She'll be angry with me."

"Why?"

"I didn't tell her I was resigning today. She knows I planned to, but..."

"I see." He scoffed. "Well, I'm sure she'll take it *just* fine. It's not like Hele to get upset, right?"

They shared a wince.

CHAPTER TWENTY-ONE

"DID MY MATE RESIGN FROM THE WING TODAY?"

Hele knew she should calm down. She knew that she should not let her temper or her worry get the better of her, particularly when she was showing up on her fearsome cousin's perch unannounced, but she couldn't help herself.

After her meeting with the witches, she'd gone to see Alex for her lunch, during which her sister casually mentioned that she'd seen Vael flying toward Taevas's perch during her morning commute. It took only a second for Hele to guess what he'd been up to.

Furious and dismayed on his behalf, she'd dematerialized and flown to her cousin's roost without hesitation. That was how she found herself standing naked before her Isand, lightning cracking behind her and hair snapping in the air.

Her cousin stepped out of the doorway and gestured grandly for her to enter the luxurious living space he used for his visitors. She'd visited just the week before, when they had their family movie night. They made popcorn she didn't eat and watched her father's choice of *"fast car movie"* — at least, that's what her mother called it.

Hele felt none of her normal cheer as she stomped into the roost, her bare feet slapping against the marble floor.

"Well?" she demanded, rounding on her cousin with mounting fury. "Did he resign?"

Taevas didn't answer. Instead, he huffed, strode over to the sunken living area, and snatched a fluffy blanket off of the cushions. Walking back over, he used quick, efficient movements to wrap her in it. When she complained, he gave her a very *dragonish* growl and sternly admonished her, "You need to calm down or you'll whip up another storm."

She didn't want to be calm. She was angry and hurt and worried for her poor mate. But Taevas was right. She didn't want to cause another storm after the one she made not even a week prior. *One storm a week is enough,* her mother had told her. *You have to learn to control your temper, tütar.*

It wasn't easy, but when Taevas tightened the folds of the blanket around her shoulders, wrapping her snugly, she felt a little bit of the bubbling anger recede. The blanket was nice. It was soft and when pulled tight, it felt a bit like Vael's wings when they embraced her.

Hele blinked, momentarily struck by the realization. *Oh. That's why dragons like blankets so much. They mimic the feeling of being held.*

Taevas ran his hands briskly up and down her blanket covered arms, like she needed warming, and said, "Now that's better. Tell me what's upset you."

Tears stung her eyes. "You can't let him quit. He has decided on it, but you can *undecide* it for him!"

"If your mate wishes to quit the Wing, then that is his choice. Mostly."

Hele hated how reasonable he sounded. Her fingers tightened in the folds of the blanket as she tried to reel in her worry. "You don't understand! Vael is so *proud* to be in the Wing. I don't want him to give it up for me. I thought I accepted it but I decided I won't. It's not right."

"I don't know if you understand how difficult it is to dissuade a dragon from doing something for their Chosen." Taevas's tone was dry and laden with centuries of experience. "I believe you and Vael are perfectly matched. You both have it in your heads that you know what's best for the other and you love to make a ruckus about it."

Hele sniffed. "I *do* know. He should not have to give anything up for me, especially when I do not know what I want to do yet."

"My sweet girl, did it ever occur to you that perhaps Vael *needs* to take a step back from his duties?"

She shook her head. "No. Why would he want that? He loves being in the Wing."

Taevas wrapped his arm around her shoulders and led her into the sitting area. Guiding her down the steps slowly, he deposited her on one of the huge, curving couches before he plopped down beside her, legs spread and arms stretched out over the back cushions.

Giving her a serious look, he explained, "Hele, your mate is a good man. One of the best I know. If not *the* best. Certainly better than me."

"But—"

"Hush now. Let me explain." It was impossible to say no to her Isand when he used *that* tone. It was deep and dark and full of a kind of dominance that made her want to shrink into something smaller. It wasn't mean or angry, but it was... heavy.

Hele snapped her mouth shut and pulled the blanket tighter around her shoulders.

Taevas patted the back of her head. "Good girl. Now, Vael *does* love the Wing. You aren't wrong. However, I've known for a very long time that his sense of duty goes beyond what is probably healthy. He thinks that he owes me his life — all of it. Once he got his wings back, he spent the rest of what should have been his childhood training to join the soldiers. Then he spent fifteen years working his way up until I made him an official member of the Wing."

His expression pinched. Hele was startled to see her normally genial, even *mischievous,* cousin look so aggrieved. The faint lines around his eyes and mouth deepened. He looked... tired. "I allowed it because I thought he needed it. I still think I was right, but that was before you." That hard, weary expression softened. "He wants to give you the time and space to find yourself. Could stepping back not give him the same opportunity?"

Hele looked down at her lap, fingers toying with the soft material of the blanket. Anxiety still prickled along her spine, but she could allow that her cousin had a point. Still, in a hushed voice she said, "I do not want him to regret giving up something so important for me, Taevas. Not when I do not even know what I want to do."

"Ah, sweet girl, that is where your Isand comes in." A claw skimmed her cheek, drawing her attention back to Taevas's slight smile. It was always a little lopsided. Her mother called it roguish, but Hele wondered if there was another reason he rarely showed earnest happiness.

In his deep, rumbly voice, he continued, "Your mate *tried* to resign, but I wouldn't let him. I've put him on sabbatical."

"Sabbatical? I don't know this."

"It means an extended absence." Taevas pushed a lock of hair over her cheek and behind her ear, his eyes crinkling. "Your mate will have his position whenever he wishes to return to it, Hele. I promise."

A shudder of pure relief ran through her. Hele's hair lost its snap. It fell limply all around them, looping over cushions and the back of the couch as she sagged, boneless, into her cousin's side. "Why didn't you say this *earlier?*" she whined.

"I enjoy vexing you." Taevas chuckled and nudged her shoulder. "Now, tell me this thing about the Collective. You do know that you could get into any of *our* prestigious universities, yes?"

Hele shifted uncomfortably. Staring at the deactivated feed screen that took up the entire wall across from them, she answered, "I know. I think I should go to school. Learning makes me happy."

"I sense a *but* there."

Her eyes swung to her Isand, who waited patiently for her to explain. Affection for him buzzed in her chest, warm and soft as the blanket he'd wrapped her in.

Taevas was not always the most agreeable man. He could be churlish, and loved to pick at those around him. According to her mother, he'd also left a legendary trail of broken hearts in his wake. He did not want a mate and he rarely took anything beyond the 'Riik's business seriously. He was dominant in an extreme way that raised the hair on the back of her neck and he tended to demand his own way in most things.

But he loved his family and his people. The fact that he took the time out of his incredibly busy schedule to sit with his distraught cousin and explain things to her was a testament to that.

After Vael's story, she also had a much greater appreciation for why he was so widely beloved. After all, her mate was not the only person he pulled from rubble.

Perhaps *he* could make sense of her conflicting desires. "I am confused because I know what I want to do, but I do not know how to do it," she confessed. "And I want to do more than that, too. I have many dreams."

"Most people do, but then again, most people aren't geniuses like you, so maybe you've got grander ambitions than average."

"Not *so* grand."

"Uh-huh. Tell me."

She peeked at him through her lashes. Choosing her words carefully, she said, "My mate told me that you united the clans at the end of the war."

Taevas's eyebrows rose, inching toward his great, swooping horns. "That's a simplification, but more or less."

"I want to do this for mine."

"You want to..." Those arched brows snapped down. A

confused frown marred her cousin's expressive mouth. "You want to unite *yours?* As in elementals?"

Hele nodded. Her stomach fluttered with nerves. She had never said the words aloud before, had only the vague desire twisted up with her other dreams, but when they were out, she felt the rightness of them in her bones. "Yes. Mine don't have clans. They don't have anyone unless they are lucky like me. Calamity had no one, and because of this he was captured and tortured and then lived without a nest for many years. I hate this."

She could feel Taevas's steady stare on her profile, but she dared not look at him when she voiced such a fragile new dream.

As if he understood that, Taevas's tone gentled when he replied, "It is my understanding that elementals are solitary, sweet girl. Uniting them might not be possible."

Hele swung her eyes up to fix her cousin with a determined look. "Maybe this is true. We are not dragons. Maybe mine will not want to live together or have nests. But they should have the choice — and they should know that someone will care if they go missing. Someone will *look.*"

There was a taut moment of silence before a huge purple hand cupped the side of her head. Hele leaned into his warm palm. His touch did not feel like Vael's, but it was comforting all the same.

Taevas stroked the swell of her cheek with his thumb and said fiercely, "I am so fucking proud of you, Hele. You bring so much honor to our clan. I hope you know that."

Her breath hitched. She could not imagine belonging to a different family, a different people. Her differences often made her stand out, but her family had always, *always* accepted her as she was.

In a rough voice, she asked, "Will you help me? I do not know how to do this."

"I will give you any resources you need, but I think you should speak to your mate about where to start. I have a feeling that together you'll have it all figured out in no time." His smile was a rare, *true* one this time; the kind that made his eyes crinkle and showed off his pearly fangs. "And maybe while you're out in the world collecting elementals, you can take some classes remotely."

Hele considered this, her excitement building. "I *will* have time while my mate sleeps."

"Precisely." Taevas leaned over to lay a smacking kiss on the crown of her head. "Now off with you, sweet girl. Go find your mate. My guess is he's probably discovered your absence and is worried sick."

She shrugged. "He's used to looking for me."

"I swear, my mate, if you keep disappearing, I am going to put a tracker on you."

No sooner had Hele materialized on their perch than Vael had his arms, wings, and tail wrapped around her. She withheld a laugh as he lifted her off of her feet and carried her blindly inside their dwelling, a low growl rattling in his chest with every step.

Hele curled her arms around his neck. "Only if I get to put one on you as well."

Vael ducked his head to nip the shell of her ear. Spark flew between them, lighting up the soft darkness cast by his wings. "If it wouldn't be a territory security risk, I'd insist on it."

"Well," she tartly replied, ire returning in a flash, "seeing as *someone* is stepping back from the Wing, that shouldn't matter, should it?"

Her mate leaned back to look at her. His hard features, so harsh and angular, were pulled tight with worry. "Hele, I—"

"I am angry with you for not speaking to me before you decided this." Hele's brows furrowed as she thought through her conflicted feelings on what Vael had done and all that Taevas explained to her. Slowly, she continued, "I am hurt that you did this and did not tell me, but... I understand. We are the same sometimes. I've thought about it and decided that I would have done it this way, too. I do not like it, but that is the truth."

Vael's head dropped. He rested his forehead against hers and closed his eyes. "I'm sorry this hurt you. I didn't want you to be anxious about it, but this... this was something I felt like I had to do — for both of us."

"Taevas explained." She stroked the back of his neck with her fingertips. The tense muscles there trembled under her touch. "He says that this is good for you, too, and that you will still have your position when you want it."

"Yes." He swallowed. "I didn't see it before, but he's right. I don't know who I am outside of the Wing, Hele. I think it will be good to find out. *With* you."

"I think this, too." She paused, weighing her words carefully, before she slowly informed him, "When I spoke with Taevas, I decided on what I want to do."

His arms tightened around her middle. "What is that?"

The words tumbled out of her, clumsy and fragile as pieces of eggshell. She explained how she did want to go to school, but how her dream of uniting her people came first. She told him how it hurt her to think of all of the elementals who did not have clans to love and accept them, and how it bit at her, the idea that so many might be hurt, or missing, all because no one thought to care for them.

Her throat tightened when she admitted that she imagined what it must have been like for *him*, trapped under the rubble. Was it not similar to so many of her kind? They could be trapped or hurt, except they had no rogue Wing, no Taevas to come save them. They had *no one*.

There is no one but me who cares. But if I am the only one, then I will have to be enough.

Vael listened silently, his chest rising and falling in a steady rhythm against hers, until she asked, "Do you think this is possible?"

Vael unwound one arm from around her middle. His hand,

warm and callused, cupped her cheek. Tilting her head back so he could look her in the eye, he replied hoarsely, "Hele, for you, *anything* is possible. Just tell me what you need from me."

"I don't know where to start. Taevas offered resources, but..." She looked away from his earnest expression, suddenly overwhelmed by the enormity of the task she had laid out for herself. "There are so many. Where do I begin?"

"Well..." Vael nudged her cheek, drawing her attention back up to his face. He smiled down at her, soft and proud and so very *dragonish*. His little gold hoops gleamed in the shadows of his wings and every one of her breaths was heavy with his spicy scent. All was still, and soft, and perfect. "Let's start with an easy one and work backwards from there."

She blinked. "An easy one?"

"Yeah, an elemental we know."

"I don't know any other—" She cut herself off. Eyes widening, Hele breathed, *"Oh.* Do you think he would agree to meet with me? The witches didn't have any luck."

Vael's smile widened into a full-blown grin. "I *think* that my mate is a determined sort of woman. He can refuse, but when has that ever stopped you from getting what you want?"

Her smile grew to match his. "You're right," she replied, bubbling excitement beginning to eclipse her worry. "I am an Aždaja, and we do not take no for an answer."

His arms tightened around her middle. "You are also an *Orlova,* and we look after our own."

EPILOGUE

AUGUST 2047 - SAN FRANCISCO, THE ELVISH PROTECTORATE

SHE WAS NOT BOUNDLESS.

Even dematerialized, her form shifted to light and heat and power, she could feel the edges of her being. She did not stretch endlessly into the horizon, nor did she float without purpose or agency.

She was finite — and more free than she had ever been.

Hele watched the massive fog bank roll in over tide and rock. The sun was setting, the air temperature was dropping, and though she had no lungs with which to do it, she held her breath.

There was a wild magic in the fog. It twined seamlessly with one another — two distinct entities that lived in symbiosis. Hele looked closely from where she hovered over one of the towers of the Golden Gate bridge, trying to see if she could spot where one being ended and the other began.

As the fog rolled ever closer, swallowing the pylons and the deck below her, she decided that she could not. This fascinated her and made her wonder, briefly, if one could tell *her* apart from a regular lightning storm.

A question for another day.

She would have to remember to ask her mate. *After.*

Hele's nerves manifested in snaps of electricity in the air. The lights at the top of the tower buzzed, glowing briefly brighter, before she got herself back under control. *Calm,* she coached herself. *Remember what minu tuli said: this is a first try. If I fail, there will be more.*

But she did not want to fail. She wanted to succeed in this almost as much as she had wanted to be with her mate. Beyond that, she just... *really* wanted to meet the being whose life had inspired her so much. She admired him. Despite the fact that they were strangers, his opinion meant more to her than she could readily admit.

He's coming!

She felt the charge in the air, that magic *shift* that was so familiar to her. Fog began to rise, creeping up over the red painted metal of the tower. It moved gracefully. She could see now why people were often taken by surprise when they suddenly found themselves in an impenetrable wall of fog. It moved so sinuously, so without obvious hurry, that it would be easy to underestimate its power.

Hele steeled herself for the conversation to come. *I am Hele Varvaara Aždaja Orlova. I live in the Draakonriik. I have my own dwelling. I have a mate who loves me. I was once vast, and even though I am now small, nothing is impossible for me. Not even this.*

Her will compressed her form, creating skin and bone from light and magic. Her bare feet settled on the cold, gritty metal of the tower just as the fog rose above the ledge.

And then she was no longer alone.

A man stood before her. He was slightly taller than she was, and built hardier, with more muscle and a stronger bone structure. But that is where their differences ended. Hele took in his pale skin with its blue undertone, his long white hair, and his black eyes with a heavy heart.

We look like siblings.

She thought of her sister, how essential she was to Hele's life. She thought of her brother Artem, how his steady support, even from a distance, helped guide her. And then she thought of this man, with his mask of indifference, and *ached*.

Who was there for him when he was lost? Where were his siblings? His clan?

Here, she thought, straightening her shoulders. *I am here now.*

"Hello," she said, forcing her voice to sound calm. "I am Hele. You must be Calamity."

The other elemental cocked his head to one side as he scrutinized her unabashedly. After several tense seconds, he replied, "Cal is fine."

"Cal." Hele nodded once. "This is better."

The smallest smile lifted one corner of his full mouth. "I agree. Why did you ask to meet me, *Hele?*" A wary light entered his dark eyes. "Most people who seek me out are after something. What is it that you want?"

Hele understood that this was why it was so difficult for them to get in contact with him. She'd tried it on her own several times, with no success. After a century of people seeking him out only to use him, she did not begrudge him caution. That didn't stop her from using her ace in the hole, though.

She gestured to the ledge before padding over to it herself. Crouching down, she dropped onto her backside and threw her legs over the edge to dangle her bare feet above the fog and the rushing vehicles it obscured on the deck below.

After a moment of hesitation, Cal followed suit.

When he was sitting beside her, his long, pale fingers curled over the metal edge and his hair moving in an unnatural swirl around his shoulders, she said, "Thank you for agreeing to talk with me. I know you do not meet with strangers often, so I am grateful."

"As my mate tells me, it is not very often that the Isand of the Draakonriik sends emails, so I did not have much of a choice in the matter."

"Still."

He tilted his head in her direction. "Still."

"I am nervous," she admitted.

Cal looked askance at her. With similar directness, he asked, "Why?"

"I've never met another elemental before."

He grunted. "I have. Briefly."

She peered at him through her lashes, terribly curious. There was so much she knew about this man and yet there were so many gaps left for her to explore. Elise Sasini's book left out much of the mundane, the things that mattered most to Hele. What were his favorite colors? Did he have a preferred food, like she did? Did he ever go to school? She wanted to know it all.

Tempering her rabid curiosity, she asked, "What were they like?"

"We are all pretty much the same," he answered, lips turning down. "Short-tempered. Blunt. Alone. That's what happens when you come into the world as we do — wreaking havoc."

Gods, her heart ached for this man. "That is not how it was for me."

Cal pinned her with a narrow-eyed look. "What do you mean?"

Hele folded her hands in her lap and looked out across the bridge, toward the tower that stood opposite the one they sat on. She could just make out the shape of a heavily muscled man standing on top, his legs spread and arms tucked behind his back in a relaxed but ready military stance. His wings, huge and talon-tipped, spread around his shoulders. The thin membrane between the bones caught the light from the lamps at the top of the tower, making them glow.

A little bit of her nervousness ebbed away. Her mate was there. Watching. Waiting. He believed she could do this and she *would*.

Sucking in a deep breath, she said, "What do you know about dragons?"

"Nothing more than what I've observed. There are a few dragons in my city, but not enough to know them well."

"I belong to a dragon clan," she told him, proud all the way to her bones. "And I am mated to a dragon."

Cal's brows rose. "You... belong to a clan? How is that possible?"

So Hele told him — all of it. Her making. Her falling. She told him how she was caught by her mate, and then how she was whisked away. She detailed her first years in the 'Riik, as well as the support she received, and then how she decided on Vael. She told him about her little apartment and then how she'd wisely given it up for the roost she now shared with her mate. She left nothing out. Not only did she have nothing to hide, but she felt like she owed it to this man, whose life story she clung to so fiercely in the beginning.

He'd given her hope and a sense that she was not as strange as she often felt. That was a gift she could only hope to someday return.

When she fell silent, Cal did not immediately fill the gap. He stared at her for several long moments, his full lips parted and eyes wide. Finally, he said in a strange voice, "You... were very lucky, Hele. The gods blessed you."

She shrugged her shoulders. "I know I am lucky. Maybe the gods have something to do with that, or maybe they don't."

Cal turned his head away. His gaze fell to some distant point beyond the bridge when he replied, "Loft's acolytes told me that I was a test from the gods. A great cataclysm meant to prove their devotion and humble them."

"I know this." Lightning snapped in response to her flare of righteous rage. "That was wrong of them. You are not a test. You are a *person.*"

His head turned slowly back to her. That tiny smile returned. "You would get along well with my mate. She says the same thing."

"Your mate is very smart and right, like I am."

He snorted. It was not quite a laugh, but very close. "Yes, my Elise would love you." He shook his head, smile dimming. "But you didn't say why you wanted to meet me. Was it just because you read my mate's book?"

"No." Hele kicked her legs a bit, buying herself a few seconds to find the right words. "I wanted to meet you because your story inspired me."

"To do what?"

She met his dark eyes, identical to her own, and answered, "I want to make a clan. For *us.*"

Cal leaned back suddenly, as if she'd landed a blow. "A *clan?*"

"Yes," she said, speaking slowly so she could not be misunderstood. "A clan of elementals. We are born alone, but we do not *have* to be alone. We can have a family — each other. That way no one will suffer when they need help, and when a new elemental is made, we can look after them. We can care for each other, like the dragons do."

She got the impression that it was not easy to surprise Cal, but she had. He sat there, fingers gripping the cold metal edge of the tower, and looked at her like he could not comprehend the words she had spoken.

Hele didn't rush him or try to over explain. She knew from her own experience that sometimes it took a while for words to find purchase in the mind, and it was not a process helped by overcrowding. So she waited, patient, and looked out across the bridge to find the form of her mate once again.

Minutes passed. Then, "...How?"

"My mate suggested the first step should be identification. We cannot help elementals if we do not know who or where they are."

Hele held up one hand and began to tick off points on the tips of her fingers, "First, we must track down and identify as many elementals as we can. Their information will be put in a secure database only open to us — things like physical characteristics, abilities, place of birth, approximate age. Next, a network. I want all elementals to have access to communication devices. I want every new being to have information on how to exist in this world — access to education, tips on overstimulation, and healthcare. No one should live in ignorance. After that, an alert system linked to m-weather units, which will alert us when a new elemental has been made."

She dropped her hand to tangle her fingers in her lap. Canting her head to one side, she continued, "Eventually, I would like to make laws to protect us and others like us. It will take many decades, I think, to accomplish all I want. But some of these things can be done quickly, if I have the right help. My cousin Taevas has offered me much, but I will need help from my own, too."

Like he hadn't heard her, he murmured, "A *family.*"

Hele gentled her voice. "Yes. It is good that we have mates, but that is not all in this world, and not all of us have Chosen. Ours should not have to if they don't want to. A mate should not be the only being who cares for you. We deserve family, too. People who will look if we go missing. People who will tell us when we are wrong. People who will love us and welcome us always, even when it is hard."

Cal's eyes took on a glassy sheen. They reflected the golden light of the massive lamps that topped the tower. That same light cast dark blue shadows across his stricken expression when he said, "A family for all of us. That is... Yes. I would like that."

Hele's heart soared. "Will you help me find others?"

"Yes. I don't know many, but I will help you as much as I can." Cal swallowed. She could see his throat bob in the dark, as if he had to force a lump down before he could speak again. "I do not need more than my mate, but... it will be nice to have a family, I think."

Hele reached over to clasp his hand. She could feel the tension in his knuckles as he gripped the edge. Aware that he did not know what it was to have clanmates yet, she told him, "We are a clan now, you and me and our mates. That means you are my brother. I will look after you, and you will look after me. We will not always get along, but this is normal. Our clan will grow. We will learn and adapt together."

His hand began to relax under hers. Each finger uncurled, just a little bit, from the cold metal edge. "What will you call it?"

"The clan?"

"Yes."

"Oh, I was thinking *Piiritu.*"

Cal's brow furrowed. "What does that mean?"

Hele tilted her head back just enough to look up at the stars and the heavy disk of the moon. In a soft voice, she answered, "It means *limitless.*"

The air *whooshed* behind her a moment before strong arms banded around her middle. Wings, huge and beautiful and imperfect, arched over her head, blocking out the worst of the frigid ocean air.

"How did it go?"

Hele leaned back into her mate as he threw his legs over the edge, framing her own. Her heart was at once heavy and full of joy. The road ahead was daunting, and the pain she knew she would have to wade through immense, but now that she had one new clanmate, she knew that there would be no giving up.

"He said yes," she answered, tilting her head back to nuzzle the underside of Vael's jaw.

One big, rough hand smoothed over her ribs and stomach with loving possessiveness. "Of course he did. I told you, didn't I?"

She pressed a tiny, electric kiss to his neck. Vael let out a low groan. "You did."

Hugging her close, he asked in a husky voice, "So what's next?"

"He invited us to dinner in his dwelling tomorrow. He wants

me to meet his mate. She will have many good ideas, he thinks. We will talk more about next steps — all of us together. What do you think?"

"I think it's an honor to be invited into his home," Vael replied. "And it can't hurt to get more minds working toward the same goal."

"I thought this, too."

"Afterward, we should fly up to see your brother and his Chosen. He'll hunt me down and skin me if he finds out we were in the EVP and didn't stop by."

Hele nodded. It would be good to see her brother, and she adored Paloma. They would have so many things to talk about, not least of which was the little dragon that would be joining their clan soon. *Well,* Hele thought, smiling, *one of my clans. I have three now.*

They were quiet for a while, each lost in their thoughts as they stared out at the rolling, billowy fog. Vehicles rushed below them and occasionally honked a horn.

"Do you miss it?"

Vael rubbed her temple with the side of his chin. His warmth blazed against her bare back, a stark contrast to the cold metal under her legs. "Do I miss what, *täht?*"

"Being in the Wing."

"A little. Mostly I miss seeing my comrades every day, as well as Taevas." He squeezed her gently. "But it's not the kind of missing that hurts, if that makes sense. I think I'll want to go back when we are ready, but for now, I am happy just being me. Being who I am when we are together."

Though she suspected as much, it eased her worries to hear it. Hele stroked the muscled contours of his arms. "Good. When you want to return, we will."

"What about you, my mate? Do you miss being what you were before?"

She wrapped her fingers around his forearms and felt his skin, his warmth, his strength under her fingers and palms. "Sometimes when I get overwhelmed, I think I do, but... but when I was *more,* I did not have you or my clans or know what love was. I did not know books, or strawberries, or swimming. Living is harder, I think, but it is also *better.*"

Hele tilted her head back to look at him upside down when he replied, "There is nothing I would not give up to have this life with you, *täht.*"

She reached up to stroke the hard, crooked line of his nose. "I would trade more eons for a moment with you, *minu tuli.*"

Vael turned his head to kiss her palm. Speaking against her skin, he whispered, "We are lucky to have this life together."

Once, she had only felt, and wondered, and decided that if ever there was a chance to be reborn into something else, she would trade her vastness for even a moment of *life.* She had drifted over the world and watched those below with envy.

They did not make sense to her, but one day she began to wish she could know what it was like to be small and strange and together with others. There was no one to hear her silent pleas, but she wished anyway.

By some twist of fate, her wish had come true. She was small, and strange, and loved beyond measure. Her boundless form had been exchanged for limitless potential — and the chance to grant the wishes of others.

"Yes," she agreed, settling back against her mate, "we are the luckiest people in the world."

THE END

A sneak peek of Burden's Bonds...

"You're not supposed to be here."

Unsurprisingly, Delilah replied without an ounce of worry. "Certainly, but I am always exactly where I *need* to be."

Kazimier Rione shot his half-sister a baleful look as she settled onto the squeaky vinyl stool beside him. As usual, The Broken Tooth was smokey and loud. The bar top was just shy of outright sticky and the music piped in through the old speakers was something bluesy.

San Francisco's premier bar it was not — and that was exactly why he liked it.

He had no trouble fitting in with the other shifty patrons, who only wanted to score a drink, a companion for the night, or a lucrative deal in a dark corner. Perhaps all three.

His sister, on the other hand, looked about as natural on the duct taped stool as an ice sculpture would in a bus station bathroom.

Even with the smoky glamour obscuring her features from all but the most discerning eyes, her bearing made her stand out. But then again, Delilah Solbourne stood out *everywhere*. It would take more than the shifting tendrils of magically conjured smoke to hide her stature, her aura of casual dominance.

And that was before one considered her outfit.

Kaz felt a headache building behind his right eye. He'd been nothing but tense for two weeks. He did not need the added stress of his sister's unannounced and *unsanctioned* visit.

"What are you doing here?" he grunted, claws tightening around the cool glass of his beer bottle.

Delilah lifted her hand, motioning for the bartender's attention. "Lemon drop, please."

"This isn't the kind of place that serves *lemon drops*, Lilah."

"Oh please, she knows how to make a lemon drop. You think this is my first visit?" She wiggled her fingers at the were woman who owned the bar.

The owner glanced over from the other end of the bar, where she'd been talking in a low voice to another were, a man most criminals in San Francisco would know on sight. He was tall, thickly built, covered nearly head to toe in colorful tattoos, and had the signature were feature: two different colored eyes. He sipped from a glass of whiskey as the bartender waved to let Delilah know she'd heard her.

Kaz let his gaze linger on the weres for a moment longer than necessary. He knew the man well, though neither would consider the other a friend.

Rasmus Adams was the enforcer of the unofficial San Francisco were pack. He was in charge of maintaining discipline amongst the weres, a people prone to explosive tempers and even greater strength, and the head of all their illegal Underground smuggling operations.

He was also a mean son of a bitch. If Kaz were being honest — something he did his best to avoid — he would have to admit that it was half the reason he liked the man.

They locked eyes for the span of a heartbeat, neither willing to be the one to look away first, before Rasmus wisely lifted his glass up in a lazy salute. It was the smallest concession to the truth they both understood: that Kaz was a far more dangerous predator than he could ever be.

Satisfied that his position was still clear in the were's mind, Kaz turned his attention back to his beer — and his sister.

"You shouldn't be in the territory, let alone in the city," he warned her. "You're banished, remember? If Teddy found out you were here, he'd have you escorted out at the end of a bolt gun."

"I am well aware." She slid him a sly look. "Are you going to snitch on me, sweet boy?"

Kaz shook his head. *Fucking family.* "Why are you *here?*"

Delilah dropped her forearms onto the tacky bar top and craned her neck to peer at the feed screen to the right of the bar. An orcish woman and a gargoyle were duking it out in a ring bordered on all sides by a frenzied crowd.

Without looking away from the screen, she asked, "How was the wedding?"

Kaz forced another gulp of beer down his suddenly tight throat. "Fine."

"Did Teddy and our girl have a good time?"

He shot her a hard look. "Lilah, I might not be as pissed as Teddy right now, but don't mistake that for apathy. You have no fucking right to call her that after what you did."

"I did what was necessary." She turned her head to look at him, but he couldn't see her eyes through the glamour. Not that it would have helped. Delilah's black eyes — the *Solbourne* eyes — were always impossible to read. He'd wondered if it was a side effect of her ability to see so many possible futures or the damage their father had inflicted on her long before any of their siblings came along.

Probably both.

"I *always* do what is necessary," she continued, sighing the words out like she was the injured party, "but I understand that it is hard to see from your limited perspective."

"Limited perspective my *ass.* You put a bomb in Margot's

fucking house. I don't care that you knew it wouldn't kill her. It *could* have."

Kaz didn't care that women tended to call him stoic, unfeeling. He didn't even mind that his own family sometimes wondered if he had any warmth at all. What he *did* mind was when one of his people was threatened.

He wasn't good for much, but he'd dedicated his life to protecting what belonged to him — and Margot Goode, his brother Theodore's mate, was one of those people.

Another witch belongs to you, too.

The thought came out of nowhere. It was a deep growl in the back of his mind, a wave of instinct and prickling conscience.

She doesn't, he growled back, ruthlessly squashing the need that fizzed under his skin. *She never will.*

"Necessity is not always kind," Delilah replied. "In fact, it is often cruel. You'll understand."

"Doubt it."

She shrugged. They both watched as the owner walked over with a sugar-dipped martini glass in hand. Kaz rolled his eyes when Delilah accepted it with a flourish, telling her to put it on his tab.

They were quiet for several tense minutes after. He nursed his beer. She took delicate sips of her sugary concoction. The match on the feed screen ended with the gargoyle's narrow victory before it switched to a new one.

Delilah was halfway through her drink before she asked with no preamble, "How long do you intend to fight it?"

Kaz's fingers flexed around the neck of his beer bottle so hard, the glass developed hairline fractures. Speaking through clenched teeth, he said, "Don't."

"I'm only curious."

He turned his head to glare at her. Aggression bunched the muscles of his arms and shoulders beneath his thin t-shirt and beaten leather jacket. "Don't you fucking dare, Delilah. I don't want or need your help."

Even if Delilah's *help* hadn't nearly killed their brother's mate, Kaz wouldn't have wanted it. He'd made his choice. It was done.

His brother had indulged Margot's wish to be married on her Coven's land just two weeks prior. Kaz accompanied them as both security and a witness, though their family did not particularly care for the Goodes, nor for the ridiculous ceremony of *marriage*.

He shouldn't have gone. He should have let his brother go with a full unit of the Sovereign's Guard instead, but he'd felt compelled to. Not simply because he loved his brother and the woman who'd saved his life just by being *born*, but because...

Well, he hadn't been able to explain it even to himself.

All he knew was that he needed to go. He needed to be there when hundreds of witches and their allies arrived to celebrate Margot's marriage. He needed to watch the flames of the sacred fire burn, to smell the incense, to hand over the groom's offering and see over his sister-in-law's shoulder—

Her.

The matte black claws of his left hand dug into the edge of the bar. Only his tenuous control kept him from ripping a chunk of the wood off as he shoved the memory of warm brown skin, dark eyes, and a soft smile from his mind.

His sister sighed dramatically and set down her glass. She leaned back on her stool to stick one gloved hand into the deep inner pocket of her short black cape. He watched, jaw clenched, as she withdrew a bent legal envelope — the kind meant to hold a large amount of paper and held closed by a metal tab poked through a hole in the flap.

It wasn't altogether *bursting* with papers, but it still had heft to it. When she dropped the bent envelope on the bar, it landed with an ominous *thwap*.

"Never fear, sweet boy," she dryly replied, "this is all the help you'll get from me. Everything else will be your choice — whether you want to accept that or not."

"What is that?" he demanded.

He wasn't sure why he asked. He *knew*. The hair on the back of his neck stood up even when he refused to look at the envelope. Instinct went from a light fizz under his skin to a full on *buzz*, like a hive of insects had been roused inside him.

"Your favorite currency: information." Delilah picked up her martini glass and took another leisurely sip. Her claw-caps, platinum and set with diamonds, winked in the dim light of the bar.

Kaz couldn't help himself. His eyes were drawn to the packet like a magnet. No matter how hard he tried to look away, they kept coming back to it. In a hoarse voice, he asked, "On what?"

"You know the answer to that."

His heart, always calm, began to beat unevenly in his chest. A cold sweat broke out on his palms. "Why would you do this?"

"Because you'll want it."

Her throat worked as she tilted her head back to toss the dregs of her lemon drop down. Setting the empty glass back on the counter, she hopped off the old stool. Her cape fluttered around her shoulders as she adjusted the gauzy white blouse she wore underneath it.

Her tone was brusque, businesslike, when she continued, "You don't want it now. I can respect that. But you will need it later." He couldn't make out her expression through the glamour, but when she lifted her head again, her inspection of her clothing finished, he knew that her face was set in hard lines. "I am not here to stop you from making mistakes, Kaz, but I'll warn you now: you are going to regret not looking."

Fear, cold and hard, closed a fist around his beating heart. "Why are you telling me this? You *never* tell us—"

"Consider it a peace offering."

"A *peace offering?*" Anger burned through some of his fear. Kazimier planted one booted foot on the filthy floor, but stopped himself from standing up. If he challenged his sister in the bar, they'd draw all sorts of unwanted attention, and he really didn't want to have to find a new haunt.

Snarling through his teeth, he said, "You shouldn't be giving me a peace offering. You should be *apologizing* to our brother."

Delilah stuck her hands into the pockets of her slim-fitted slacks. "I won't apologize for doing what needs to be done. You'll accept it. Teddy will, too."

"Lilah, I—"

Quick as lightning, she was only inches away. If she hadn't been kin, one of the women who raised him and trained him, Kaz would have gone for her throat as soon as she moved. As it was, he sat ramrod straight, his lip curled over his prominent fangs, and allowed her to brush strands of his hair behind his pointed ear.

"Sweet boy," she whispered, leaning in to press a kiss to his cheek. "Tell your brother and his wife that I said hello."

Just as quick, she turned around and walked away.

Kaz watched her tall figure cut through the smoke to reach the flier-covered door. Even drunk, people hastened to get out of her way. They might not have been able to tell who she was, but there was no hiding that she was an elf.

And even if they didn't recognize that, only the dead wouldn't fear Delilah Solbourne.

A nudge with her silver-tipped boot pushed the door open into the warm night. He watched her slip out, the buzzing in his ears disguising the uneasy murmuring that followed her exit.

The door swung shut. His eyes darted away, back to the packet on the bar.

It sat there, innocent, bent nearly in half, and taunted him with what he could never have.

Without his permission, his hands strayed to the envelope. His mind rebelled. He knew he shouldn't look. Looking would only make the compulsion worse. It would only make the obsession he could feel budding in that dark part of his mind that much stronger, more resilient to extermination.

But he couldn't stop himself.

His fingers, large and callused from years of fighting and handling weapons, shook as he fumbled with the little metal tab.

He held his breath as he lifted the flap. Tugging the papers out just an inch, his eyes snapped to the no-nonsense black text.

His heartbeat thundered in his ears. Cold gripped him again, the burning sort of fear that stole the breath from a person's lungs.

Kaz gnashed his teeth and shoved the papers back into the envelope.

But it was too late. The words were branded into the backs of his eyelids now. He could see them every time he blinked. When his heart beat, he swore he could *hear* them, each word keeping time with the unsteady *thump-thump, thump-thump.*

She was in him, her name seeping through his veins like a saccharine venom.

Atria Le Roy.

ALSO BY ABIGAIL KELLY

Find all new releases, bonus chapters, and exclusive content on the Works by Abigail Patreon!

FRAGILE BEINGS: A NEW PROTECTORATE NOVELLA COLLECTION

In the first volume of The New Protectorate Stories...

Fate can't be contained.

#376: A fey Changeling is rescued from captivity by a reluctant demon on a quest to find his fate. Of course Dom expects trouble, but he is shocked to discover his fate is tied to an imprisoned fey woman. Charlotte's a kicking, spitting, hissing little Changeling — and she's his.

A dragon's kiss burns cold.

Astray: When Paloma Contreras, arrant scientist, accidentally dooms a rogue dragon to death, she'll do anything to save his life. If that means giving up the mountaintop she's called home her entire life, so be it. Too bad Artem Aždaja has no plans to steal her roost. He only wants one thing: *her.*

Desire fogs the mind.

Weathering: Elise Sasini, an intrepid reporter and weather witch, sets out to uncover the story of San Francisco's legendary sentient fog and gets a lot more than she bargained for. The mysterious elemental agrees to tell his story in exchange for a taste of the life — and the woman — he craves.

Three novellas. Three couples. One fractured world. Step into a magical near-future where love builds, breaks, and defies boundaries.

Available in Kindle Unlimited, ebook, and paperback!

Consort's Glory: The New Protectorate
Book One

Margot Goode, healer extraordinaire, knows that being noticed is the fastest way to getting herself murdered — or worse. But even with a secret like hers, she can't stay cloistered forever. On her own in San Francisco, she's on the hunt for the one person who can stop her magic from turning against her in a catastrophic meltdown.

Margot doesn't expect things will be easy, but even *she* is surprised when someone plants a bomb in her Healing House, nearly killing her and wiping out her anonymity in one fell swoop. Attacking a healer is an egregious breach of the laws that keep the races from war. Attacking Margot Goode, granddaughter of the terrifying Goode Matriarch and leader of the most influential coven in the country, is not just blasphemous — it demands retribution.

Theodore Solbourne, newest sovereign ruler of the largest Elvish territory in the West, has waited his entire life for the woman he will one day claim as his consort. With the power to keep her finally in his grasp, he's planned their meeting down to every last detail... only to have all the carefully crafted steps in their courtship blown away when she's nearly killed before he can even say *hello*.

With her life and his kingdom on the line, there's no time for subtlety. Earning the trust of the woman he's been mad about his entire life just became much harder: the speculation of war is sweeping through the city, a goddess's acolytes call for justice, and a traitor's shadow looms over his household. But nothing, not even Margot's single-minded determination to keep him out, will stop him from winning her heart.

Available in Kindle Unlimited, ebook, and paperback!

COURTSHIP'S CONQUEST: THE NEW PROTECTORATE BOOK TWO

Their future hinges on a promise.

In the wake of her mother's death, Camille Solbourne is determined to follow through with her deathbed promise to arrange a union with a suitable partner and get out of the Solbourne family. A union is cold, more business than love, and negotiating them is a dangerous political dance. It's not what she wants, but sometimes happiness is found in compromise – and keeping one's promises.

Their choices haunt their past.

Nearly twenty years ago, Viktor Hamilton, alpha of San Francisco's lone coyote shifter pack, let his mate go. Becoming someone his pack could rely on for safety and guidance is the only thing that kept him sane in the long, lonely years that followed. When the opportunity to make a life-altering choice for the betterment of his people arises, he makes a promise to see it through.

What he doesn't expect is for the world to change around him in the blink of an eye. After a volatile run-in with Camille reignites the flame between them, he knows he can't leave the past alone. The only thing standing between them is their fraught past and Camille's furious determination to tie herself to another man. Pursuing Camille means gambling with the future of his pack, but Viktor won't let his mate go a second time – even if it means he has to put his life on the line to keep her.

Available in Kindle Unlimited, ebook, and paperback!

GLOSSARY

A full character directory and map can be found at Abigailkkelly.com

PLACES

United Territories and Allies: What we would consider the continental USA. A loose federation of sovereign states established after the Great War. The UTA capital is United Washington, in the Neutral Zone.

The Elvish Protectorate: Also known as the EVP. Stretches from Oregon to New Mexico. Capital city is San Francisco. Led by the elvish sovereign Theodore Thaddeus Solbourne.

The Coven Collective: Also known as the Collective. Encompasses Washington state. Capital city is Seattle. Led by a large coalition of witch covens, with Sophie Goode acting as their leader.

The Orclind: Encompasses much of the Midwest. Led by the Iron Chain, a close-knit government made up of orcish clans and family groups. Capital city is Boulder.

Shifter Alliance: Takes up a section of the midwest and all of the south. (Unfortunately includes Florida.) Run by a very, very loose alliance of shifter packs from three capital cities — Minneapolis, Oklahoma City, and Atlanta.

The Draakonriik: Also known as the 'Riik. The second smallest territory, it takes up all of the Great Lakes region and stretches to New York. Led by Taevas Aždaja, the *Isand* (ee-zand) of the dragon clans. Pronounced: *dra-kon-reek*

The Neutral Zone: Also known as the New Zone. Technically it is held by a coalition government consisting of representatives from the UTA, but in reality it is run by a syndicate of feuding vampire families. It is a small strip of land squeezed between the Draakonriik and the Shifter Alliance.

GODS

Light & Darkness: The primordial gods who created all the others. Also known as The Lovers and First Union. Both are generally represented as female.

Loft: God of the sky and creator of flying beings. Twin sibling to Tempest. They know no gender. Also known as the Boundless One.

Tempest: God of the ocean and creator of all water beings. Also known as the Hungry God and the god of love.

Burden: God of the Earth, creator of all beings who live within it — most notably the orcs. Husband of Glory.

Glory: Goddess of sunlight, magic, and creator of elves. Worshipped by witches for giving the gift of magic to humanity.

Blight: God of forested places and disease. He works in partnership with his daughter Grim and shares her dominion over demons and all reviled creatures.

Grim: Goddess of death. Known as the Merciful One and the Brilliant Lady. She is widely beloved.

Craft: God of change, newness, and messengers. Creator of humanity and viewed warily by non-worshippers as the Chaos Maker. They change their gender frequently, but generally is referred to using he/him pronouns.

TERMS

Alpha: a broad term used by many communities generally associated with a leader — either of a small family group, a pack, or even a territory.

Anchor: a vampire's mate. Anchors are carefully chosen and usually longterm-to-permanent arrangements, as they take considerable energy to make/become. A vampire must inject their venom into a host many times before their blood chemistry adjusts such that they become unsuitable for consumption by another vampire and their sleep cycle switches to a nocturnal pattern. At this point, they can can also produce/carry to term a vampiric child. Temporary anchors do exist, although they are relatively rare due to the intense withdrawal symptoms associated with ending the regular venom intake.

Arrant: someone born without m-paths, or the ability to channel and use magic.

Change: an elvish term for a sudden shift into adulthood. This is marked by 5-14 days of "madness", usually triggered by some stressful event around the age of 16-18. The elvish body is flushed with hormones to the point where sudden growth, overwhelming hunger, and aggression take over. Viewed as an incredibly vulnerable time, only immediate kin are charged with the care of their loved ones — which includes isolating them, preventing harm to themselves/others, and feeding them. The change marks the second phase of an elf's life, when they are no longer coddled children but young adults who can accept challenges and family responsibilities. Formal adulthood is attained at 30.

Changeling: a term first used to refer to fey children fostered out to non-fey homes, now more widely used to mean any person raised by people who are not the same beings. *Ex:* A dragon couple raising a human child.

Chosen: the formal term for a dragon's mate. The act of finding a mate is called *Choosing,* and is considered sacred.

Consort: an elvish mate. A term used exclusively by elves to refer to someone they are biologically compelled to pair up with. This usually involves intense sexual attraction, but can vary from person to person.

Dragon: a person with a dual form. In their bipedal form, they have claw-tipped wings, horns, and a tail. In their quadrupedal form, they are roughly the size of a standard SUV and can fly at extremely high altitudes for weeks at a time. They come in a variety of extremely saturated colors that shift with the time of day (light to dark). They breathe cold blue fire and can see the Earth's magnetic field. Identifying mating feature is marked change in behavior, including the overwhelming urge to nest.

Elemental: a being created by a spontaneous magical eruption. They often take on the attributes of whatever weather they happen to be born into, *i.e.* a lightning storm might produce a lightning elemental, or a blizzard might make a snow elemental.

Empath: a person with the ability to feel and manipulate the emotions of others.

Elf: someone born with jewel-toned skin, claws, pointed ears, and four fangs. Very secretive and considered apex predators who require a strict hierarchy to function. Average height of 6-7ft. Identifying mating feature is the retraction of claws.

Fever: shifter mating imperative triggered by the "animal's" choosing of a mate. Marked by a perpetual near-shift — elevated body temperature, increased aggression, build-up of magic, and the compulsion to mark. A shifter displays their readiness to find a mate by creating a den.

Fey: a person with nearly vestigial, insect-like wings, small fangs, and claws. Usually live in large groups. Identifying mating feature is bioluminescence.

Foresight: the ability to see multiple possible futures. The average number is between 2-4, with the likelihood mental instability increasing with each subsequent possible future.

Halfling: the elvish term for an elf with mixed heritage.

Healer: a person who possesses the ability to see into and heal bodies through touch.

Isand: the title of the leader of the Draakonriik. Pronounced *ee-zah-nd*

M- : *M-* is frequently used as shorthand to denote when something is infused or otherwise combined with a magical element.

Marriage Sigil: a custom symbol branded into the foreheads of spouses (pairs or multiples). Each one is unique and infused with a small amount of magic as a reminder of the power love holds. They are typically sought out by worshippers of Glory — mainly witches and arrants. Elves, though worshippers, don't usually take a marriage sigil when they find their consorts or form a unions with other elves.

Mate: a catchall term for a significant other. Used by many cultures, it has varying degrees of weight. To shifters, orcs, and demons, the word mate is synonymous with family, monogamy, and dependence. It is much more loosely used within arrant society, as well as amongst elves, who generally prefer the term *consort.*

Met: acronym for *magically enhanced tech.* A branded home assistant that can do everything your Alexa can, as well as small, low-level magic to help around the house.

Metallurgic Inoculation: a vaccine given to all elves within hours of birth to make them immune to iron poisoning.

M-siphon: a containment device used to imprison a magical being and siphon off their magic. Highly illegal.

R-siphon: also known as *reverse siphon.* New technology that redistributes magic away from the siphon instead of into it.

M-lev: a play on *maglev,* meaning a high speed train that levitates using magnets. In this case, magnets *and* magic.

M-weather: magic weather. Very common, but can result in "clusters" or storms that wreak havoc if not properly contained. In rare circumstances, it can also produce a sapient being known as an *elemental.*

Orc: a person with green, gray, russet, or blue skin, two fangs, and claws. Widely renowned for their strength and beautiful voices. Identifying mating feature is "the kohl", or altered, dark pigmentation of the hands and feet developed after meeting their mate.

Pixie: a small, winged creature with compound eyes with about the same level of intelligence as a rat. In the wild they live in trees and in burrows, but have adapted to living in walls, pipes, mailboxes, etc.

Pull: elvish mating imperative. A sudden hormonal shift caused by exposure to a compatible partner's pheromones, marked by the retraction of claws and volatile mood shifts. The pull is only "satisfied" when hormone binding occurs — the term for long term exposure to a mate, resulting in permanent biological dependence on their pheromones. This process increases fertility and often results in the conception of multiples. Lack of exposure to a mate can cause severe physical reactions (lack of appetite, muscle pain, headaches, insomnia) as well as the deterioration of mental stability.

Shifter: a person who can shift into an animal form. They can partially shift (changing only parts of their bodies at will) and often take on characteristics of their other half. Famous for their strength and tenacity, as well as their dual-voiced "shifter purr" which many people find deeply attractive. Usually found in packs.

Sigil: a symbol used to channel magic. Western countries use the alchemical alphabet formally codified in the 1800's, though many, many variations are used all over the world.

Sovereign: the title of the ruler of the Elvish Protectorate. It is capitalized when used in place of a name.

Turbo Virgin (c): Theodore Thaddeus Solbourne, Sovereign of the Elvish Protectorate and Head of the Solbourne Family.

Union: an elvish marriage. Usually done for financial, political, or procreational benefit. The parties involved are not fated or biologically compelled to be with one another, and might have many lovers or even a consort outside of their union.

Vampire: a person who drinks blood to survive and cannot go out in sunlight. Vampirism can only be "caught" with the exchange of fresh blood, and as of 2045 is much more widely spread through procreation. Vampires can only breed with their *anchors*. Identifying mating feature is marked change in behavior, including overwhelming desire and need for total isolation.

Ward: a magical barrier with varying levels of protection. A ward can be something as simple as a proximity alert — "someone walked into my garden" — or as complex as full on defense — "someone crossed the threshold and has now burst into flames". The severity of the ward depends on the complexity of the sigils used to create them, and wards can have many layers, each one with a unique purpose. Personal wards can also be used, such as in clothing or embedded into jewelry, though they tend to be expensive and difficult to foolproof.

Were: a person infected with the were virus, a much mutated strain of the vampirism virus, resulting in altered physiology and magical ability. They can be identified by their heterochromia, or different colored eyes. They are the newest magical race and viewed warily by the general public for a variety of earned and unearned reasons. Identifying mating feature is marked change in behavior, including highly increased territorial instinct and the urge to nest. Pronounced *ware.*

PRONUNCIATION GUIDE FOR NAMES OF IMPORTANT CHARACTERS IN THIS BOOK

Hele: heh-lay

Aždaja: ash-DIE-ah

Vael Orlov: vay-le ohr-lohv

Alexandra: ahl-ex-an-d*r*a (rolled *r*)

Artem: ah*r*-tem (rolled *r*)

Paloma Contreras: pah-low-mah kon-treh-*r*ahs

Taevas: tay-vahs

Constantin: kohn-stan-tin

Valerie: vahl-uh-ree

Atria Le Roy: ay-tree-uh luh roy

Ruby Goode: roo-bee good

Jacques du Soleil: zhah-kuh doo so-lay

Calamity: kuh-lam-ity (prefers *Cal)*

ABOUT THE AUTHOR

 Abigail Kelly is a writer and illustrator of alternate histories, love stories, and women with drive. Her work is heavily influenced by both her modest family roots and her passion for history. She is also a bookseller at an independent bookshop where she gets to badly influence impressionable young minds and put her favorite books in eager hands, as well as the host of the Kingdom of Thirst podcast, a show all about romance novels and why they matter.

Her favorite authors are Shirley Jackson, V. E. Schwab, Ursula K. Le Guin, Kresley Cole, Nalini Singh, and just about anyone who writes about the weird and wonderful. She lives in San Francisco with her dog, Babs, who remains stubbornly illiterate.

CONTENT WARNINGS

Content warnings: Miscommunication/language learning, culture shock, adoption, experiences of war, parental death (past), virginity, and explicit sexual content.